LIBERTY IN THE KABASH

A REEL TO REEL ADVENTURE

A NOVEL BY GEORGE PALMER

This is a work of fiction. Names, characters, places, brands, media, and incidents are either the product of the author's imagination or are used fictitiously. The author acknowledges the trademarked status and trademark owners of various products referenced in this work of fiction, which have been used without permission. The publication/use of these trademarks is not authorized, associated with, or sponsored by the trademark owners.

Copyright © 2015 by George Palmer

All rights reserved. Without limiting the rights under copyright reserved above, no part of this publication may be reproduced, stored in or introduced into a retrieval system, or transmitted, in any form, or by any means (electronic, mechanical, photocopying, recording, or otherwise) without the prior written permission of the above copyright owner of this book.

First Print Edition: December 2015
Library of Congress Cataloging-in-Publication Data

Palmer, George
Liberty in the Kabash/George Palmer – 1st ed
    ISBN – 13: 978-1518810817
    ISBN – 10: 1518810810

1. Liberty in the Kabash—Literature & Fiction
2. Literature & Fiction—Sea Adventures

10 9 8 7 6 5 4 3 2 1

For all the good shipmates.

"If the boy and girl walk off hand-in-hand in the last scene it adds 10 million to the box office."
George Lucas

When asked by his relief the name of the evening flick during patrol 58 aboard *USS John Marshall* ... "Russians dyin' in the snow."
D.A. Smith TM2 (SS) USN

"Everything I learned I learned from the movies."
Audrey Hepburn

"Give me a couple of years, and I'll make that actress an overnight success."
Samuel Goldwyn

"The brains of members of the Press departments of motion-picture studios resemble soup at a cheap restaurant. It is wiser not to stir them."
P.G. Wodehouse

"Any submarine lieutenant worth his salt
can operate a movie projector,
and those who want to make lieutenant commander, had better
damn well be able to do it with one hand, and in the dark!"
P.D. Tomb RADM USN RET

"Darling the legs aren't so beautiful,
I just know what to do with them."
Marlena Dietrich

CONTENTS

Forward	I
Chapter 1 – Sam I Need You!	1
Chapter 2 – Change of Plans	18
Chapter 3 – Approved Anchorage	28
Chapter 4 – Sightseeing with Mustafa	37
Chapter 5 – A Critical Error	44
Chapter 6 – Le Jardin d' Essai	50
Chapter 7 – The Dupe	60
Chapter 8 – A Special Invitation	65
Chapter 9 – Hot Reelin'	73
Chapter 10 – Wajid's Taxi	80
Chapter 11 – An Early Departure	89
Chapter 12 – Diplomacy	105
Chapter 13 – The Kasbah	113
Chapter 14 – Fate Intervenes	120
Chapter 15 – Underway Again	129
Chapter 16 – Ready for Turnover	138
Chapter 17 – Friends in Need	148

Chapter 18 – What Else is a Senator For?	158
Chapter 19 – Let's Go Home!	168
Chapter 20 – Letters	177
Glossary	183
Acknowledgements	190

FORWARD

EVERY SAILOR WHO'S EVER BEEN to sea on a navy ship knows what a great boost to morale a motion picture can be. They help break up the day and they let the viewer *escape* from the watch routine and *imagine* any number of things. Comedy, tragedy, sci-fi, western, action-adventure, romance; you pick the genre, sailors immerse themselves in whatever movie is shown. It doesn't matter where; the mess decks in a submarine, the wardroom of a destroyer or the chief's mess on a carrier, the evening "flick" is something that sailors look forward to all day.

USS Hornet's crew remembers watching Dorothy Lamour, Hope and Crosby in *The Road to Singapore* as Halsey led them deep into the Emperor's backyard to launch Doolittle's Raiders on their storied attack in April of '42. There are tales of men aboard WWII submarines holding their breaths watching Ginger Rogers in *Kitty Foyle* during the lulls between Japanese depth charge attacks in the deadly South China Sea. Movies helped them forget the war and imagine themselves somewhere else as the picture rolled.

Since 1919, Hollywood has been entertaining the navy with a movie exchange program. Initially run out of the old Brooklyn Navy Yard, the Navy Motion Picture Exchange system has handled them all, 16 mm films back then and DVDs now. New films are released under license and the navy provides them to ships and stations at no charge. The only rule is: make sure you return the film in the same condition as you received it.

GOD HELP THE SHIP that loses a reel of a movie! The chances of *ever* getting another decent flick after that kind of screw-up are precisely zero. A ship with that hanging over its head had better get used to using their projectors to show "hand-shadow" puppets forever. Take it from me ... I've been there. This *is* a novel but ... oh what the Hell, you'll see.

CHAPTER 1
SAM I NEED YOU!

YN3 SAMANTHA WILSON HAD THE afternoon off and she wanted to use that time productively. She had already finished her weekly letter home and had also finished her Spanish lesson with Lieutenant Walsh. She was boning up on her languages before their next port visit. Carrie Walsh had quickly volunteered to help her of course, her duties as a nurse in *USS Dwight D. Eisenhower's* sick bay allowed her plenty of time to drill her friend in the language. Two hours of conjugating Spanish verbs was actually not as boring as Wilson had initially thought it might be. She just had to remember that it would make it much easier to get around in Tangiers if she could actually ask her questions in the local language.

Her morning had gone well and she'd finished all the routine correspondence for the captain by 1100, she had even found time to work up another installment of the ship's history. She had taken over that responsibility when the captain had seen that their PAO was not doing an effective job of maintaining the required narrative. It had to be submitted every January to the "little old lady in tennis shoes" that was cognizant of such things for every ship in the navy, at the old Navy Yard in Washington DC. Wilson had totally redone the work that the PAO had fumbled and she ran up a new entry every week. Her latest installment had covered their participation in the battle group's "sinkex" and their excellent liberty port visit at Palma, Mallorca. The captain had been so pleased with her narrative that he'd even designated her as his Ship's Historian. It wasn't a real billet of course, but she thought it might look good in her last evaluation, the one that would close out her enlisted service record when she transitioned from enlisted to midshipman-in-training status. The PAO had been given additional duties in the operations department to make up for the diminution in his workload. Wilson hoped it was something fun.

She had even grabbed an early lunch and had time to trade news and scuttlebutt with her friends on the mess decks. She was still dawdling over the last few spoonfuls of her Jell-O when AB3 Stephanie Turner stopped by her favorite mess table to talk to her.

"Are you Sam Wilson?"

"Yes I'm Wilson, how can I help you?"

"I'm Stef Turner and I understand from someone in the signals gang that you know everything there is to know about getting an officer's commission."

Wilson laughed, "Stef sit down, if you have a minute." She pointed to an empty seat and waited for Turner to get comfortable. "I don't know all the ways for an enlisted woman to get a commission but I know the Seaman-to-Admiral Program's way. I was accepted for the naval academy and I leave for Annapolis after Thanksgiving. The captain is going to release me after we return to Norfolk in November. There are other ways too, maybe you should see Miss Olson, the educational services officer, I'm sure she has all the different information on them. Come to think of it, you could stop by my office later this afternoon and I'll let you look over the BuPers Manual sections that apply. All the qualifications and prereqs are listed and there are lists of all the required paperwork and the timelines for submission. It's not hard but you need to look over the program paper and there are things like; how long you may have to extend your current enlistment to have enough time to participate in the various programs."

"That would be great Sam! I can come by between 1500 and 1600 if that's okay with you."

"Sure Stef I'll be there, do you know where my office is?"

"No I don't, aren't you in the main ship's office?"

"No I'm in the captain's yeoman's office. It's two doors down from the captain's cabin and right across the passageway from the captain's mess pantry door. It's well marked."

"Wow, I've never been near the captain's cabin before maybe I should put on my dress whites before I come to see you!"

Wilson laughed, "Not necessary Stef, working sailors come to see me all the time. Wear your dungarees, that'll be fine. And listen, think about why you want to be an officer in the meantime."

Turner looked thoughtful as they got up and took their trays to the scullery. "See you later Sam, I have to go inventory towing gear and hold-down straps."

Wilson went back to her office and found that the afternoon COD flight had delivered a stack of new mail that she would have to sift through. There were quite a few official items and she found several letters from families of the crew who had written the captain with various requests and suggestions related to their loved ones who were under his command. She knew he would like to see those right away and she set aside the ho-hum navy mail in favor of taking the personal ones to him.

When she knocked and announced herself, Captain Christensen had her come right in. "What do you have for us this afternoon Sam?" He was smiling as she came in and placed the opened stack of letters on his desk.

"Some 'crew family' letters captain. I think you'll enjoy the one from Mrs. Carbury right here on the top of the stack. I think she's concerned about her daughter Pamela. I pulled her information, she's a SHSN and right now she's assigned to the ship's laundry." She peeled the top letter off the little pile and he took it from her.

Christensen furrowed his brow, "Hmm West Brimfield Ohio. Ah I see, her mother is concerned she may not be getting enough fresh air and sunshine because she works 'deep inside the ship'. I wonder if she wrote her folks that or they just surmised it? Well in any event, I'm appointing you to look into her situation and see what's up, before we write back to her folks."

Wilson smiled, it was the first time he had tapped her to personally look into a shipmate's individual situation. Usually he would have given it to the command master chief or tasked a department head to look into the matter, she hoped it meant that his confidence in her abilities was growing. She smiled again, "Captain I'll go find her this afternoon before chow, I'll be able to advise you in the morning before the department head meeting Sir."

He chuckled and nodded as she turned and left his cabin, she was a silver bullet and he knew she would have a good idea of what to do in the morning.

Wilson got back to her office just as her language teacher arrived. Today's lesson was to be 'getting around' in Español. They practiced "train talk" and "taxi speak" and she learned how to pay and make change in dinars, centimes and pesetas. They even had time to take on registering in a hotel and ordering some basic food items at restaurants. Walsh was happy with her progress, "Sam your pronunciation is improving and your memory for the verb tenses is really good. Tomorrow we'll do the casual phrases you should know for on-the-street conversation: asking directions, stops on the bus line, help with a map, all those kinds of things. You are really doing well! It took me three years of high school Spanish and then three in college to really get it well and you are doing wonderfully after only a few days, Magnifico!"

Wilson was still laughing when Walsh left just as Turner appeared in her doorway. "Hi Stef come in and sit down I'll pull out the things we need."

She took the copy of the BuPers Manual down from her bookshelf and put the thick volume on the table, flipping it open to the section on officer programs. "Here we go Stef pull up that other chair and we can sit side by side and look over the material."

Turner sat down and Wilson began, "First, of all are you between 17 and 23?"

"I'm 20, I've been in the navy for two and a half years and aboard here for most of that time. I'm single and I'll be eligible to take the second class exam next spring."

Wilson nodded, "Okay, no previous college credits and not taking any of the available college programs?"

"I was going to start a couple of courses this month."

"Okay then, are you not eligible because of any physical problems, and how have your quarterly marks been?"

"I'm physically fit that's for sure, I haul heavy straps and hold downs around on the flight deck all day. My evaluations have been pretty good too, I think I'm thought of as a 'three point nine and then some' sailor."

"Well that seems to cover most of the bases and it means you could go either to the naval academy or into the navy enlisted science and engineering program. That's seaman to admiral and both programs provide a four year college degree followed by commissioning and you get paid while you're in school."

Turner laughed, "College and a job afterwards!"

Wilson frowned then, "Remember I asked you to think about why you want to be a navy officer? What did you come up with?"

"That's easy Sam, I love the navy and I love my country, I think I have a lot to give back and I can do that better if I advance, get a commission and have more responsibility."

Wilson thought that she had said just the right thing. "Stef I think you are going into this for all the right reasons, why don't you start by talking to your division officer as soon as possible? I'll make a copy of this check sheet and you can start by filling in the forms you'll need and getting the recommendations from your division officer and the others in the chain of command that you'll have to have so the package can be sent off to the bureau. Don't worry though, when it comes to the captain's final signoff and letter, if Captain Sweeney gives you a thumbs up, it's a done deal. I'll look for the package because I'll probably have to write the captain's recommendation letter."

Turner had one question for her, "Sam when does the selection close for the year?"

"There's a BuPers notice that sets the dates for each year because they have to work this process in with all the other boards and things that have to go on in the navy. I can't tell you the cutoff date for this year but they have it at the ship's office. Ask YN1 Mitchell for it. But if you miss the time for this year it will be all set for next. Let me know if you need any help with it Stef." Wilson unfastened the binder clamp, took the check sheet from her BuPers manual and ran two copies for Turner.

"Here you go Stef, I made you two so you can use your copy and your division officer can have the other. It should help move things along. My advice is find out the cutoff date and then set up a schedule to finish everything, your goal should be to finish all the paperwork and get your internal review board completed at least two weeks before the cutoff. We'll still have to mail everything back to the bureau and that takes a week or so."

Turner nodded and smiled, "Thank you Sam, it's great that you could take the time to advise me. You're the expert at this as far as I'm concerned."

Wilson laughed, "I was lucky with mine, the captain is my boss so it was easy to get the review part done. In fact, I didn't even have a board of officers interview me and the captain got me advanced to third class early so I could qualify. I'm pretty sure he just wants to get rid of me!"

Turner giggled, "I doubt it Sam. Hey nice work on your Navy Marine Corps Medal! I was in the front rank when you got it and I was proud to be another *Ike* woman sailor when you did!"

"Thank you Stef, that means a lot to me, coming from another *Ike* woman. By the way, how did your inventory go?"

Turner laughed, "Well I found a bunch of handling straps that had frayed wires and some were even beginning to rust under their protective coatings. The master chief wasn't real happy with that because we'll have to order a bunch of new ones, but in the long run maybe it may prevent some accident or incident down the road. I went to QA-school before this Med run, so I knew pretty much what to look for."

"Excellent! See that's what I like about being on *Ike*, everyone does their part; no one's job is too little or too unimportant. I think that's really the secret of the navy. Little things matter. Hey I have to go down and see to something in the laundry, but after that I'm free until chow time. Maybe you could show me some of the things in your department that have to do with your job. Captain Sweeney is always talking about pendant cables and arresting gear cables at the department head meetings, maybe you could show me some of those."

Turner smiled and nodded, "Sure Sam, meet me on the hangar deck by the starboard elevator in about an hour and I'll give you the cook's tour. See ya then!"

She departed and Wilson locked her office to go investigate the Pamela Carbury situation. She found the red-haired seaman in the midst of dumping sheets and pillowcases into a giant laundry cart and loading it into the biggest washing machine she had ever seen. Carbury and another seaman had pulled the seabag-sized bags of soiled sheets over to one of the huge running washers from a room-sized pile of similar bags. Each was marked with a specific division name and they would be picked up by junior personnel in those divisions and returned to their berthing compartments for reissue after laundering. Individual personal laundry bags were stuffed inside other giant bags, each was marked with the owner's name and division. Wilson was impressed, the sailors in the laundry did a fantastic job as far as she was concerned. She'd never lost even one garment due to mix-ups or carelessness in her whole time aboard *Ike*. The worst that had happened to her clothes was a smashed button on one of her dungaree shirts. It was noisy and warm but well ventilated in the big compartment, and Carbury and her fellow SH seemed to be working well and they weren't sweating.

When Carbury stepped away from the open door of the washing

machine Wilson made herself known, "Hi are you Pam Carbury?"

The young seaman looked up, "Yes, is there a problem? Did we lose one of your socks or something?"

Wilson laughed, "No it's nothing like that. I'm Sam Wilson and I was just interested in how the laundry actually gets done so I came down here to find out from the people who actually do the work." She gave her a big smile, "How do you like the job? I suppose it gets boring doing the same thing every day. But it is such an important job, keeping all the sailors on *Ike* in clean uniforms."

Carbury shrugged, "I never thought about it quite like that. I think the chief is going to rotate me out of the laundry and into the dry cleaning plant after our next port visit. For my money that will be a blessing, especially since there isn't much call for dry cleaning at this time of the year. Our whites all get washed. Of course next month we'll shift back to blues and I'll have a big load then. Still, it's something new. I'll be glad when I get to rotate into running the ship's store."

"When does that happen Pam?"

The other laundry person spoke up then, "The chief has us in rotation so that we each spend three months in the laundry, then three in the dry cleaning shop and last, three working in the ship's store under instruction. After that we can get a shot at the barber shop or one of the other tasks aboard."

Wilson nodded her understanding. It seemed like a fair arrangement to her.

Carbury shrugged, "We work six on and twelve off watches here in the laundry. Right now everything is fine and no one is overworked because all four of the washers and dryers are working, but last week one of the dryers was out of commission. It backed up everything. Did you notice you didn't get your things back 'til a day later last week?"

"Yes Pam but that didn't really bother me, my job isn't one of the hot and sweaty ones where I'd need to change uniforms a couple of times a day like the poor nukes or the guys in the air department. I do remember the supply officer saying that something was broken on one of the dryers and the engineer officer sent two of his EMs to troubleshoot and fix it."

Carbury was impressed, the supply officer was her department head, a full commander, "When did you talk to the supply officer Sam?"

Wilson smiled and shook her head, "Oh I didn't, but he was telling the captain during the department head meeting, I was there taking the notes. I'm the captain's yeoman, and I came to see you because I wanted to know if you are okay doing your job. Your mother sent the captain a letter and it seemed to me that she's concerned that you aren't getting enough fresh air and sunshine aboard."

Carbury was mortified, "My God! My mother is such a worrywart! But I can't believe she wrote the captain! I'm so embarrassed."

Wilson was quick to jump in, "Pam don't be, it's okay my mom was concerned for me when I first came aboard but I wrote her and explained the job I do and the things that go on aboard and I tried to make it sound upbeat. She understood too and I usually send a letter every week to let my folks know how I'm doing here on the ship. Listen, the captain will want to know you're really okay, so why don't you come and have chow with me this evening, I could even introduce you to my friends, would you like that?"

"Sure Sam I'd like that. I get off at watch change that's at 1800. I could meet you on the mess decks then."

Wilson nodded, "I'll meet you right at the entrance to the mess decks, I have head of line privileges and I'll get you in with me. After chow I usually go to the gym with my friend; unless you have something else to do, it would be fun if you could come with me."

"Gosh I'd really like that! I don't seem to get very much exercise. I could change and shoot some baskets with you and your friends."

Wilson laughed, "So you're a basketball star Pam?"

Carbury smiled proudly, "I don't think I'm a star or anything, but my team won the state championship for middle-sized schools when I was a senior. I was the point guard."

"Excellent Pam! You know, we have enough women on the ship to have a women's basketball team. Why don't we talk with the command master chief and see if we can set up something. I know he was pushing for a basketball league back in Norfolk. You could be a pioneer in navy women's sports! Hey I have something to do for a little bit now and I have to meet someone on the hangar deck to learn something new, but I'll meet you on the mess decks at 1800."

Wilson headed back to her office then. She had a few things to look up and she thought she could satisfy the captain's faith in her by letting him know that her new friend was embarrassed that her mother had written the letter of concern and she had a plan to make her mother happy. She sat down at her word processor and banged out a first draft of the captain's answering letter, she made it short but very sweet and assured Mrs. Carbury that Pam was fine, in good health but eager to shift from the laundry to the dry cleaning plant when it was her turn. More importantly she would be a key player on their new women's basketball team. After she looked it over she added one more touch. She had the captain assure her that he would be sitting in the stands at the tipoff for their first *Ike* women's basketball team game rooting for Pam and her teammates.

Wilson gathered several other pieces of mail that were waiting to be opened and scanned their contents. One was important enough to bring right in to the captain so she took that with the letter to Seaman Carbury's mother and knocked on the captain's door. "Captain it's Wilson Sir."

"C'mon in Sam, what have you got for me?"

She pushed open his cabin door and stepped in, "I think this will work for Seaman Pam Carbury Sir. I talked with her in the laundry and she's a little homesick but she's in the regular rotation that the other SH strikers are in and she's embarrassed that her mom wrote you. I also have her starting in our new women's basketball team so she should be getting some exercise. Here's what I came up with to send her mom, I think it will work and she's going to write a letter of her own this week."

Christensen took the letter she handed him and scanned it quickly, "Perfect Sam, thanks. What else do you have there?"

"It's from the bureau Captain," her huge grin gave it away. "Congratulations Captain, I'm so happy for you! You're screening a year early for rear admiral selection!"

He took the letter from her and saw that it was from his detailer, congratulating him on that very significant achievement.

He laughed, "Thanks Sam, this is great news! I'll bet my wife already has the word though, via the wives' circuit. I'm probably the last to know." His face took on a somber look then, "Sam please don't mention this to anyone, I don't want anyone to get the idea that I'll be leaving the ship before it's my time to go."

She was crestfallen, "Oh Sir, I can't agree with that! I know everyone aboard thinks you're the best captain they've ever had, and when they hear that you are getting an early look they will think it's because you surely deserved it. If they take you away from us to go on somewhere else, well that's only to be expected. Please Captain, let me tell my friends and I'm sure the XO already knows too."

Christensen thought for a moment, it wouldn't make a bit of difference actually, the word would be out soon anyway. "Alright Sam go ahead. Thank you for making me think about it."

"Excellent! Thank you Captain!" She was bubbling over with joy for him. He certainly deserved to be an admiral. He would be a fantastic one! "Boss I have to go meet someone on the hangar deck now if you don't mind but I had figured out the Seaman Carbury thing and I just opened your bureau letter and I wanted you to know. I'll see you in the morning Sir."

She met Turner at the starboard elevator, "Hi Stef show me the ropes! I can tell you that I've seen all the things you and the handlers have to do from the bridge but never up close. I've always wanted to do that."

"Come on then Sam I'll show you what we do."

For the next hour she showed Wilson how they loaded a plane

onto the elevator and brought it from the hangar deck up to the flight deck. Wilson put on a blue handler's vest and hearing protection to ride up with the A6. They moved it up onto the deck, towed it past the other secured planes, backed it into it's assigned slot aft of the island, and fastened it down there. Wilson got to sit beside the first class AB who operated the heavy tow tractor, the "mule", as the plane was moved. Afterward Turner showed her to the "Deck Boss's Model Room" where the big scale model of *Ike's* flight and hangar decks was faithfully maintained. Phone reports and closed circuit TV cameras enabled the watch to track it all. Every plane and every major deck component was tracked and every movement of every plane was quickly planned out in three dimensions, in advance, to prevent traffic jams and tie ups. During flight ops, the deck boss's rapid management of safe plane movements on deck was vital to the ship being able to fulfill her mission.

Wilson had heard about the model room efforts from the air boss of course, his reports during the department head meetings with the captain had often mentioned the cameras and how they helped his department perform. It still amazed her though, that the hundreds of men and women in the air department could be so carefully coordinated and choreographed. She had great pride in them all.

"Gosh Stef, thank you for letting me have a peek at some of the things that go on in the air department. I know I haven't seen all the maintenance efforts, and there were no launches or recoveries this afternoon, but this was great! I feel like a real working member of the crew right now!"

Turner giggled, "Sam thanks! It was fun showing you around. Maybe some time you can come help do the deck wash down with all of us. If you want I'll find out when we're doing it again and let you know."

"I'd like that Stef. Hey are you free to come have supper with me? I'm meeting another girl for supper at 1800 and I think you'll like her. We're going to the gym afterwards and you can come along, you're tall, can you handle a basketball?"

Turner and Carbury both joined her on the mess decks and Wilson led them to her favorite table. They joined several of her other friends who had arrived minutes before.

"Everyone this is Stef Turner and Pam Carbury. I just met them both this afternoon. Pam works in the ship's laundry and Stef moves the planes around on the flight deck." She introduced her old friends, "This is Bad Billy Bates the most fantastic boxer in the fleet, he takes the first class bo'sun's mate exam in the spring and this is HM2 Judy Obenauf the best corpsman in the battle group. This is Terri Holden she's been my mentor aboard *Ike* for the last six months, you probably recognize her from the liberty launches; she just finished her Cox'n quals when we were in Piraeus in June. This is Abby Reynolds, she's in the engineering department and she's due to be advanced to fireman next month."

After the introductions they began enjoying their supper as they bantered back and forth. All were in fine fettle with the end of their days' work, and those who had been keeping track of their deployment were able to report that they now had less than fifty days to go until they would return to Norfolk.

Wilson saw the opportunity, "So Billy what's the first thing you're going to do after we get back home?"

Bates smiled and looked into her laughing green eyes, "I'm takin' Judy home to meet my mom and dad. Then I'll have a decision to make after we get back from Pittsburgh. My PRD is in January and I have to decide where I want shore duty. Most billets open for Bo'sun's Mates ashore seem to be around navy yards. I'd like something a little more broadening and enriching if I can find something, and most of all I don't want to be very far from Judy."

Wilson smiled as her friend finished his wish list, "Maybe there's a way to do both things Billy." She turned to Obenauf, "Judy when is your PRD? Have you thought of rolling off at the same time as Billy? Maybe you can get the same duty station."

Obenauf nodded smilingly, "Yes Sam we thought of that and as long as Billy goes to a duty station where they have a naval hospital or a clinic we could make it work."

Wilson nodded back, "There must be oodles of places like that, why don't you check the available billets document in the ship's office? I'll bet there are a ton of listings that would be ideal for both of you, right on the east coast."

Obenauf was about to say something when they were interrupted at their meal by the arrival of the one person who could get all their attention simultaneously. Command Master Chief Connolly was certainly an impressive looking sailor. Six foot three and ramrod straight, his crisp khaki uniform looked like it had just come from the dry cleaner's within the last two minutes.

Wilson wondered which of them he wanted to talk to. She saw him at least twice a day when he stopped by her office on the way to see the captain. She was on very good terms with him, the result of mutual respect for each other's hard work.

They all fell silent as the master chief began, "Good evening everyone I don't want to interrupt, but there's a rumor someone wants to start a woman's basketball team aboard."

He was grinning and looking right at Wilson so she answered, "Yes Master Chief, there are at least three girls right at this table and I'll bet that if you put it out on the TV we could expect twenty or more girls at tryouts if we hold them tomorrow after evening chow. Oh and I think I can find us a coach too. If we get enough women coming out we can have two teams and scrimmage against each other until we can find a ship or station that wants to play against us. I'll bet *Ike's* women's team could be the nucleus of a league."

"You sold me Sam, I'll get some uniforms made up but I want someone to help design them. Also I need a favor."

Wilson couldn't believe he was asking *her* for a favor. There were four thousand other sailors on *Ike*, six if you counted the air group, what could he *possibly* need from her? She gave him a tentative smile, how hard could it be? "Sure Master Chief, how can I help you?"

"You've heard that there's to be a 'ship's entertainment night' after we get to Rota and hold the 'outchop' brief with the *Independence* battle group that's coming over to relieve us."

"Yes Master Chief, the captain mentioned that there's supposed to be a play or something and he wanted a lot of the crew and the officers to participate. He said you were coordinating it, but I don't know anything more than that."

Connolly flashed her a grin, "Well I am coordinating, in fact if we were in Hollywood right now, you might say that I'm producing the show. Do you know what the producer's job is in a movie Sam?"

Wilson knew something was up but she played along, "Isn't the producer the one who puts together the funding and buys the 'property'? Doesn't he hire the actors and the crew?"

"Very good Sam! But there's one very important item that you left off the list and that's hiring the director, the person who will tell the story and get the most out of the actors during the production. That's why I'm here now, Sam I need you!"

His plea caused all talking at the table to cease and the silence spread to the nearby tables as dozens of their shipmates strained to catch the actual words that the august presence of the senior sailor aboard was sounding in the middle of the mess decks.

He grinned again and Wilson had a feeling that she was about to be sucked into the middle of the master chief's diabolical plot. When the words came they were almost overwhelming, "We're doing a comic opera and we'll have a big cast, an orchestra and the most expansive stage production that any ship's company ever put on. We'll film the show and it'll go down in the history of the navy as the best crew's entertainment ever produced. I'll be the Cecil B. DeMille of the carrier navy and you'll be the Sam Spielberg of it all, right along with me. I'm hiring you as the director of the show. You'll audition the players and hold the rehearsals and you'll have full charge of the production. I'll get the scenery and the stage set up for you and you can tap any department or division for anything you need, but you're it! Now here's the score and the script."

He handed her the folder-sized pamphlet with its buff-colored cover. *HMS PINAFORE*. "A light comic opera in two acts" by William S. Gilbert and Sir Arthur Sullivan.

Wilson took the packet from him and goosebumps broke out on her forearms. She had at least a passing familiarity with the comic opera and fragments of its tunes began rattling around in her mind: Little Buttercup's aria, Sir Joseph's classic *"When I was a lad I served a term…"*, the crew's opening ditty *"We sail the ocean blue and our saucy ship's a beauty…"*. This could be the most fun thing she'd ever been involved in. But she knew there would be a ton of work involved and she would have to find the time to make it all happen. Suddenly it seemed like it might be too much and she almost wished the master chief had chosen someone else.

It was almost as if he were reading her mind and he grinned at her, "Sam I've already cleared this with the captain, in fact it was the captain that suggested you. Don't forget you can have as many assistant directors as you need and we'll have someone handle the music. I'll have every one of our shipmates who have instruments aboard come to your auditions too. So let me know what you want for scheduling auditions and I'll give you one of our crew's lounges for a headquarters."

Wilson could see there was no way out, she'd been drafted so she might as well make the best of it and maybe there was a silver lining inside this cloud, perhaps she could find a person who could take over her job as captain's yeoman. She had been thinking about that lately, she'd be transferred as soon as they got home and she had to make sure the captain was well provided for. Her relief would have to be smart, able to take shorthand, have excellent typing skills, but most importantly have a good attitude and personality.

She smiled then, "Master Chief you drive a hard bargain I'll make up a cast and crew list and build an announcement for the XO to put in the plan of the day in the morning and we'll run it on *Ike* TV. I want to be well into rehearsals by the middle of next week." She eyed the striking master chief and pictured him in a blue uniform, heavy with gold braid, sporting a big fore and aft hat with plumes. "Master Chief I think you'd make a fine Captain Corcoran, can you carry a tune?"

They finished their meals and Wilson led her friends to the gym, a few quick rounds in the ring with Bates would help clear her head and then she would be able to set her priorities: basketball team, normal duties, Spanish lessons, the letter to Carbury's mom and now this play! She would need at least two assistant directors and she had an idea who would be good. She donned her head gear and pulled on her boxing gloves. "C'mon Billy let's do this! I've got a thousand things to do and I need to be in the right frame of mind."

Bates blocked her first two punches, he could tell from the way she was attacking that her mind was working at flank speed. She was dangerous when she was like that.

CHAPTER 2
CHANGE OF PLANS

"WHAT'S THE MATTER SIR?" WILSON saw the look of wide-eyed wonderment on the captain's face and recognized that something was up.

"Our next port visit has been scotched Sam, apparently there is too much unrest for us to risk having liberty in Tangiers. We've been switched to *Algiers,* you know I'm almost ready to bet that some moron in the State Department couldn't figure out the difference or made a whopper of a typo".

He handed her the message he had just scanned and she saw that indeed they were now slated to visit Algiers, Algeria for a week, in company with *Porter* and *Montpelier.* The dates were the same as those originally scheduled in Tangiers. Well she had better let her friend know that the Spanish lessons weren't needed any more. She'd have to find someone to help her learn some French too if they were *really* headed to Algiers.

She wasn't worried about the upcoming port visit though, their port visits so far in the Mediterranean had been safe and almost uneventful if she didn't count the almost disastrous stranding in May, or the rocket attack in June, which had almost hurt her friends. The only sad part of their upcoming port visit was that her love wouldn't be able to be there with her to enjoy the exciting sights of the city or the exotic foods in the Algerian restaurants. Her fiancé Ron had been flown back to the states and was now in the pipeline to enter the naval academy. She had his latest letter on her desk. He had even enclosed a snapshot of himself with two of his roommates at Naval Academy Prep School. He was smiling in the photo and obviously feeling quite good dressed in a football uniform. He wrote that he was studying hard, and that took up most of his time, but he had still had enough to make the football team. His jersey number was clear in the photo, number 14, the same as his old high school number when he had been quarterback on their very successful Southwest Valley High Timberwolves a few years back. Gosh he was handsome in that uniform! She missed him so much but at least she wouldn't have to worry about him, he was safely engaged to her and with the demands of school he would stay out of mischief. He wrote to her at least twice a week, such beautiful letters!

The department heads filed into the mess and took their seats for the morning captain's briefing as Wilson sat by the XO waiting for the captain to begin the meeting. She knew it wouldn't take long this morning and she was glad, she had a million things to do after she cranked out the status sheets. She had to recruit her assistants and get started in putting together the plan for the ship's comic opera. She knew they only had a month and a bit to spare to be ready and a week of that time would be spent in Algiers. She would have to factor in the time that her cast would be spending ashore. It would be hard to hold a rehearsal with most of her cast members ashore wandering around the city. Her head was still spinning with plans and questions that needed answering before they began the work ahead.

The captain was just announcing the change in their port visit and she wondered if he had any other last moment information to add and he did, "Alright everyone I'll turn the rest of this meeting over to Petty Officer Wilson who is the director of the entertainment we'll put on when we're at anchor in Rota next month for turnover. She's taken on this extra responsibility so that we can host the crew of *Independence* and give them something to laugh about on the front end of their deployment. Go ahead Sam, tell them what you're doing."

It was as if he'd dropped a lead weight on her as she sat there but she recognized the twinkle in his eye and gulped before she stood and began, "Well as the Captain just remarked our 'entertainment' is no small undertaking, I'll be putting notices of our audition schedule in the plan of the day and on *Ike News and Views* today but you should take back to your departments that I need both men and women who can sing. We're doing *HMS Pinafore,* some may know it as: *The lass who loved a sailor* it's the classic story of a ship captain's daughter who was sought as wife by England's First Sea Lord. I know you'll remember his '... *polished up the handle on the big front door'*."

She paused in her excited presentation as the air boss, Captain Sweeney, hummed and drummed his fingers on the table in the tempo of the well-known tune.

"Aha! Perfect Captain Sweeney, I'm looking for a Sir Joseph who can really get into the part!"

Every one of the other department heads laughed and she went on to describe her other needs; "I'll need a Captain Corcoran, a Josephine, a Buttercup, a Ralph Rackstraw, a Billy Bobstay, a 'Midshipmite', a Bo'sun, a Hebe and a ton of sailors as well as a passel of sisters, cousins and aunts for the chorus! We'll begin the auditions this afternoon and everyone is welcome to come try out. I have to get organized but I can promise that everyone who comes to try out will have fun. The small crew's lounge near the mess decks will be 'Pinafore headquarters'. So if anyone has suggestions for candidates, get them to me at my office or to one of my assistant directors who are Lieutenant Walsh in the medical department and Lieutenant Bishop the Flag Lieutenant. The command master chief is rounding up the people for the orchestra so all your people should know that too. That's really all my news on it but believe me, it will be a fun night and no one should miss it."

They were all still laughing and chattering about the promised entertainment as they filed out of the mess. The engineer officer followed her to her office and she hoped he would volunteer for one of the roles, she thought he had a very distinctive speaking voice and wondered if he could sing too.

"Sam I came to suggest you talk with MMC Owens. He's a tenor and I've heard him singing in the engineroom, he's quite exceptional. I'll have him swing by this afternoon."

She smiled, "Thank you Commander, I need all the talent I can get."

She had to hurry with the notes she was transcribing but finished just in time to scurry off to meet the ship's TV channel personnel. They would tape her announcement of the show and her plea for crewmembers to come later that afternoon for auditions in the crew's lounge. She made sure to pin back her hair and put on fresh lipstick before she went for her TV debut.

She gave the woman chief photographer's mate, who interviewed her in front of the camera, a 3X5 card with the list of cast characters on it. She had only to ask Wilson what she was looking for in a Sir Joseph or a Buttercup. Wilson gave the details in her sunny enthusiastic manner. "I'm looking for a *very* mature, precise and knowledgeable male singer for my Sir Joseph. Someone who's the image of a Knight of the Bath, a man who truly *could be* the ruler of the 'Queen's Navee'. But I'll confess that I've already ruled out the command master chief, I'm thinking of him for a special part. Now as far as my poor little Buttercup goes, Chief you could have a lock on that part. Let me hear you say 'tobaccy'!"

She also got in her search for a French tutor and was just in time to join her friends on the mess decks for lunch where Billy Bates was already tuned up to have some fun with her. "Well Sam the first lieutenant was all over us this morning. He said that if Bill Bobstay and Dick Deadeye don't come from the first division he's cancelling our liberty the whole time we're in Algiers. So I want special consideration if I come to try my hand at singing."

"Not a problem Billy," she laughed. "I know what you can do already. You just have to work on your Brits accent. I had you picked as my *Bobstay* last night in the ring."

A line of people was waiting outside the crew's lounge when she arrived after lunch. She posted the rehearsal call schedule she'd typed up on the bulkhead and distributed copies of the score and the script around the table the master chief had set up for her. Two crewmembers were already there with their guitars and she gave each of them a copy of the score. They would be the accompanists for the men and women who were trying out for the parts. The master chief came in then and handed her a list of shipmates and the instruments they played. "Sam you'll have an orchestra made up of three guitars, two horns, an accordion, a flute, a violin and a drummer. Also Lieutenant Commander Kendall, the flag secretary, said she could help as orchestra leader, she'll be stopping by sometime this afternoon to check in with you. I almost forgot, there is a first class aerographer's mate that you should look at for Hebe or at least one of the aunts. Beautiful voice, her name is Parks."

Wilson was impressed, the master chief seemed to be able to wrangle just about any kind of help she would need. She had already lined up MS1 Sims, the captain's mess supervisor, as her third assistant director and her nurse friend Carrie Walsh was already sitting down to coach some of the women shipmates who would become Sir Joseph's sisters, cousins and aunts. She saw her friends Abby and Terri looking over the score for the chorus. It took an hour and a half to get through the line of sailors who were trying out for the four "jolly Tars", she had already picked the fifth, her Billy Bobstay. She thought Bates would be funny as a black bo'sun in the Brit navy. She and Lieutenant Bishop had just agreed on the other four Tars. Chief Owens came in a few moments later and Wilson handed him the score for the first of the Captain Corcoran songs, "*My gallant crew ...*" and welcomed him, "Hello Chief we've been led to believe that you have some enviable vocal skills! We sure need a *right good* captain!"

The chief laughed nervously, "The engineer told me I had to come and try out with you Wilson but I was hoping for just a bit part maybe in the chorus."

Wilson smiled at him, "Chief the captain's song is really a round between him and the chorus of his crew. Can you read music?"

"Sure Sam I was in the chorus in high school."

"Good, go ahead and try this, just do the captain's lines, we'll put the chorus with you later."

One of the guitar players played the right cord and the chief began, "MY GALLANT CREW GOOD MORNING". He was *wonderful* and even Lieutenant Bishop was impressed.

By the end of the afternoon session they had cast all the roles except for Sir Joseph and Ralph Rackstraw, the sailor who would become the captain's daughter's suitor. Wilson had made a list of the dozens of other things that had to be done. She had Sims go find the chief in charge of their tailor shop. He took with him some sketches that she'd made after looking over old photos of British sailors in the ship's library. She enlisted the chief in charge of the carpenter's shop to help her draw up a set that he and the men in the shop would build. There were props to get and arrangements to go over for the musicians and she was at a loss for how they would get everything done in the short month or so they had before they would anchor at Rota and put on the show. She hoped she'd be able to pull everything together and make it all happen on opening night. It was only when Seaman Reese, who they had picked as Tom Tucker the "Midshipmite," called out ATTENTION ON DECK that she was jerked from her thoughts.

Admiral Townsend walked in smiling and joking with the men and women in the lounge, "Stand easy everyone, I just stopped in to see if there's a part for me. Sam how are you doing? I watched you on the TV earlier and I thought I'd come down to offer my services. What are you still trying to cast?"

Wilson's heart leapt, here was her almost favorite sailor in the whole world and he had taken the time from his busy schedule to come and see her. She had already shanghaied two of his staff to be directors and several more had parts as cousins and aunts, but Admiral Townsend was *just* what the doctor ordered! Wilson put on her best sign-up-right-over-here smile and the words just popped out of her mouth, "Blimey it's the Monarch of the Seas, Sir Joseph Porter KCB!"

The other cast members began the cheering then and the Admiral knew he'd better at least accept the part with good humor. He hadn't been set up at all, he'd just walked in and fallen into the trap. "Sam you drive a hard bargain and I want you to know that I may not have the best voice in the world but I'm game to try, there'll be times that I can't make rehearsals though."

Wilson was smiling from ear to ear, "Of course, Sir Joseph, and that's what understudies are for! I have Master Chief Connolly tabbed to be your understudy already, it's the least he can do after all. And don't worry Admiral, I'll make the rehearsals so we'll be able to concentrate on the parts you're in when you're available. I was hoping to begin tomorrow morning right after quarters with the sisters and the cousins and aunts, and then on the afternoon watch, work on the opening with the Tars and the sailor's chorus before the captain's "Good morning" number. I wouldn't need you 'til about 1700."

"Done Sam. I'll be here on the dot!"

The rest of that evening was taken up by a whirlwind of actions and questions from the cast members and the master chief stopping by to let her know her orchestra would be available right after morning quarters. He had juggled watches with the senior watch officer and there were few in the crew who didn't realize that the production, and getting everything ready to put it on, had a priority just under conduct of the ship's mission. Sam Wilson had only to snap her fingers and people would jump to and get the most trivial or monumental things done. The master chief told her that the men of the first division had her picture pasted on the bulkhead on the fo'cs'l!

During chow on the mess decks there was a constant stream of well-wishers who stopped by to see if they could do anything to help in the workup to the biggest deal aboard. Even some of the men and women from their air group offered to help, Wilson just got a taste of what it must be like to be the director of a big screen motion picture. Wherever she went, people she didn't even know greeted her with smiles and "high fives". She was the most famous sailor in the battle group already because of her notoriety in saving her friends from their marooning in May and her medal ceremony during their Mallorca port visit. She even had some of the men in their helo squadron asking for her autograph!

After dinner she and Bates went to the gym for their evening workout and found that ringside was crowded with shipmates who had come to watch their spirited sparring. Wilson saw that Chief Owens and most of her "Tars" were in the front row cheering and laughing as she and Bad Billy took to the ring. They began a chant that grew as the two boxers started their circling, "BOBSTAY, BOBSTAY, SAM, SAM, SAM, BOBSTAY, BOBSTAY, SAM, SAM, SAM". Bates started laughing and Wilson joined in as the chant was taken up by more and more of the crowd. Wilson thought, "If only they love the show as much as they like the boxing it should be a *rousing* success!"

It was certainly the most widely attended sporting event that *Eisenhower's* crew ever gathered to witness. They settled down to spar after the "fans" quieted down and the workout took the last of Wilson's energy for the day. She knew she would sleep soundly all night.

The whole week was a whirlwind of meetings with her assistants to work out their problems and celebrate their successes. The uniform shop had made the blue dress coat for Sir Joseph so heavily draped with gold and decorations that Admiral Townsend joked that he'd have to work out, just to be able to lift his arms. The striped shirts for the Tars and the members of the chorus were fabulous and the SHC that ran the shop turned out to hail from New Hampshire, he was from a French Canadian family and was glad to tutor her before their port visit. The men in the carpenter's shop had done miraculously in building and painting their *Pinafore's* quarterdeck.

Chief Owens turned out to have more than just vocal skills, he was an accomplished dancer too and he choreographed the opening number with the sailor chorus and Tars, a dozen fine young men and one woman in striped shirts and bell bottomed trousers happily pretend-swabbing the deck while singing; *We sail the ocean blue and our saucy ship's a beauty!*

Wilson was even able to find a yeoman she could groom to relieve her as captain's yeoman. SN Marta Fernandez had come aboard on the return COD flight that had taken her sweetheart to the naval air station in Rota Spain, the first part of his journey to the naval academy. Fernandez had just graduated from YN A-school and Wilson tweaked the system and had her assigned to her. She wasn't yet capable of the rapid shorthand that had made Wilson the most sought-after scribe in the battle group, but Wilson had her practicing for two hours every morning. She assumed her position between her and the XO during the department head briefings and attempted to keep up with the flow of information she heard coming from the captain's senior officers. She wasn't familiar yet with the technojargon that the air boss or the engineer and reactor officers spouted, but she was a quick study. Wilson had confidence in her and used the positive reinforcement techniques she had learned from the captain and Admiral Townsend to help her improve. With continued practice she thought she'd be able to handle all the captain's correspondence by the time they returned to the states and she was detached. Wilson even leaned on her to take over much of the filing and typing duties so she could spend more time in her role directing the show.

By the middle of the second week the orchestra could play the whole program without a mistake and the cast only needed minor cueing. All the major arias and the chorus had worked out the kinks and Wilson thought that the show could go on in a week or so and they would be a hit. They still had to work out makeup and they would wear their costumes when they were all tailored. The first slow walk-through dress rehearsal was set for the day after their port visit in Algiers. Now if only that went smoothly, no one caught a horrible cold or fell down a companionway and broke his leg, there was an end in sight.

CHAPTER 3
APPROVED ANCHORAGE

IKE WAS SAFELY ANCHORED AND her swing against the current had stopped, leaving her pointed directly at the beautiful, high dome atop the basilica of Notre Dame d'Afrique in the center of the old port city. Wilson could see the first of the launches pulling away from the pier and bound for them. These would contain the Algerian officials who would want to see their medical certifications and board them to discuss the various regulations they would have to follow when their liberty parties toured the city. It was all old hat to her. Next they would have to help *Montpelier* and *Porter* tie up alongside them here in the outer harbor. She knew her friend Bates was leading a group of bo'sun's mates who would do that job as soon as the approaching gray destroyer and the sleek black submarine were quietly alongside, *Porter* to starboard and *Monty* to port. The plan was to nest together as they had done in Mallorca so they could mutually support each other. *Monty* had no small boats of her own but *Ike* and *Porter* would more than take care of her needs with their many liberty launches. The three ships were all different but when they were together it seemed to her that they made an incredibly effective, cohesive team. Of course she had a less than objective interest in the two ships approaching *Ike*, her best friends were serving aboard them. It would be wonderful to see the sights of Algiers with her old neighbor from Iowa, Ted, and his beautiful sweetheart Dorothy. Gosh she couldn't wait to see them again!

She was intent on watching the topside party on *Monty* as she crabbed in towards their port side at the slowest speed her throttle-man could choke her powerful engines down to. It seemed that the gap between the two mighty nuclear powered warships was closing at glacial speed. Wilson wished the current would help them, she could see the hulking figure of her friend Ted in his dungarees and a bright orange lifejacket, just forward of *Monty's* sail. He would surely be happy to finish mooring, she could already picture his silly, crooked, grin as they talked about old times on the farm over a glass of milk on the mess decks with his adoring fiancée, Dorothy, at his side.

"Another twenty minutes Sam." The captain's estimate nudged into her thoughts, "We're ready to receive their mooring lines now and as soon as they're safely alongside we'll send over the gangway and their power cables. You can have lunch with your friends onboard as soon as you like."

She giggled, "Gosh Captain it just seems so natural having *Monty* on one side of us and *Porter* on the other. I just wish that Ron could have stayed with *Porter* another month or so, it would have been wonderful to share the sights here with him."

"How's he doing Sam, do you hear from him often?"

"Oh yes Captain, I got a letter just the other day from him. He's playing football with the NAPS team. I think he said they would scrimmage the academy frosh sometime this week and their JVs next week."

The captain chuckled, "Sounds like he's plenty busy then. It's been a lot of years but I can tell you when I was at the academy it was fast and furious but fun too. You'll be joining him before you know it. How's your protégée coming along? How much of the load is she carrying for you now?"

Wilson laughed, "She does all the typing now Captain and I have her understanding the important mail pretty well, she's almost there in her shorthand too, but I'm still not satisfied with her manner, her personality. I want her so that when the department heads come to the morning meeting she'll be the bright spot in their day and they'll all leave with an 'it's-gonna-be-a-great-navy-day' feeling. Sort of 'Iowa sunshine in a bottle'. She's from Phoenix though but we're working on it."

Captain Christensen was laughing as he got up from his bridge chair to come and look from the port bridge window down at the *Montpelier* as she edged in closer. Half her sail was blocked from sight as she neared the overhang of the flight deck; in moments it would totally obscure the view. No one on the bridge could see the activity under the high wide deck. Only phone reports from the men on the weather deck, just below the flight deck, kept them appraised of the situation. By all accounts, the line handling was proceeding smoothly, the first lieutenant had put one of their RHIBs in the water earlier to transfer a few of *Ike's* BMs to *Monty* to assist in the mooring, her friend Billy Bates was in charge. Finally they could see nothing of *Monty's* deck or sail at all, she was totally overhung by their high flight deck as the line handlers overcame the resistance of wind and current working the sides of the two great ships in together side by side.

Christensen had only missed the exact moment by a minute, *Montpelier's* captain raised *Ike* on UHF just then and thanked them for the highly professional work that Bate's team had provided in their mooring and proffering an invitation to lunch aboard. "*Montpelier* this is *Eisenhower*, I'd suggest we wait on that luncheon until tomorrow, instead I'd like to invite you to lunch with me in my mess, I have *Porter* and the Admiral joining me already. There's a quick port brief at 1000 in my mess and we can have lunch after that."

The reply was instantaneous, "Accepted with pleasure Sir, I'll be there when you want me."

Wilson knew that the visiting captains and the admiral would be available after the meeting and she'd have a chance to introduce them all to her little protégée then. It would be good training for her. Afterward she would escort her aboard *Monty* and *Porter* to introduce her to her friends. Poor Marta was so shy and she was in awe of even the most junior of officers, Wilson wanted to broaden her circle of friends, it would help her gain more confidence and she wanted her to be able to handle all pay grades of officers by the time she relieved her. It would make her captain's job much easier if the others knew that she was capable and always there to keep the burden of administrivia from bogging him down.

Porter was securely tied alongside to starboard half an hour later and the meeting in the captain's mess would begin as soon as the boarding officer and other Algerian officials arrived aboard. Wilson could see the launch bearing them underway, halfway between the landing and their anchorage. A small Algerian flag streamed from its stern marking it as an official craft. A second small unmarked boat got underway for their anchorage too. The captain thought it might be the official from the American embassy they were expecting. There were two gray French warships tied to the quay wall, a large destroyer with a big boxy stern with her smaller corvette consort, their tricolors wafting back and forth lazily in the tentative sea breeze. The salutes began as soon as *Porter* was moored with them, *Ike's* saluting battery was answered by booming from the harbor, and from the big destroyer which was wearing a broad command pennant.

Wilson secured from her sea and anchor detail station when the word was passed throughout the ship and hurried to her office. Her protégée was there finishing the last of the outgoing mail for the captain to handle before he had to meet with the others. "Okay Marta, let's get to the captain before he has to welcome his guests, and make sure you have your best smile ready for them."

The captain signed the six outgoing letters and then they quickly filed into his mess to take their places against the bulkhead behind him, ready to take any notes needed during the meeting. The command master chief escorted the Algerian officials and the embassy man into the mess moments later and Commander Cushman, from *Montpelier*, followed them into the room. Commander Gavin, from

Porter arrived next, and Wilson heard the unmistakable voice of Admiral Townsend chuckling with his chief of staff as they came down the passageway. She jumped to her feet and sang out, "ATTENTION ON DECK" just as the admiral strode into the mess.

Everyone was on their feet as he greeted them with his "As you were everyone." He shook hands with the two just-arrived ship captains, the two Algerian officials and the attaché from the embassy. He was about to take his seat when he spied Wilson and her young apprentice smiling from behind Captain Christensen. He walked around the table smiling as he took the young woman sailor's hand. "So you're the young lady who is good enough to fill the shoes of the best captain's yeoman in the navy! Tell me your name Seaman."

She almost gulped but managed to squeak, "I'm Seaman Fernandez Sir, Marta Fernandez."

"Glad to meet you Marty, I'm sure I'll see you around a lot. How long have you been working for Sam here?"

She smiled, "For just two weeks Admiral, I'm still learning the ropes."

The admiral chuckled, "Well Marty, you couldn't have a better teacher. The rest of us have been working for her for a lot longer than that!"

His comment drew a burst of laughter from the captains, it was just the touch needed before they sat down and got to the business of their briefing.

The briefing officer was very efficient and his precise, though accented English, was easy to follow. Algeria was a Texas-sized country, the second biggest in Africa, and the two million inhabitants lived mostly around the coastline. Algiers contained by far the biggest portion of their people. There were areas of the city where it was just plain unsafe for the visiting American sailors to roam, but by far the population was friendly and there were many fine shops, sights to see, and things to do. The principal merchandise items available in the shops were local clothes, Persian rugs of all sizes, and metal work, mostly ornate bird cages. There were many fine restaurants serving French-inspired cuisine and there were an equal number of Moorish establishments.

There was a small building at the landing which would be made available to the visiting ships for use as a shore patrol headquarters. *Ike* would set up a radio communications network between the ships at anchor, the SP building and the embassy. The meeting lasted an hour and invitations to attend welcoming dinners at the presidential palace, the embassy, and the city hall would be reciprocated aboard *Ike*. Wilson scooted off with her protégée to transcribe and make copies of the notes and schedule as the captain's mess attendants poured fresh coffee for the conferees.

Seaman Fernandez was visibly excited as a result of the meeting and the atmosphere that surrounded it. "Wow Sam, when I was in YN A-school they taught us the basics and I understand them of course, but no one said anything about being around important officers or foreign dignitaries. I've seen the admiral before from a distance but I never expected he'd ever shake my hand or compliment me or anything. He sure seems like a wonderful gentleman."

Wilson laughed, "He's *my hero* that's for sure! He's the one who went way out on a limb for me and the others who were lost back in May. You're in great shape now too, he just hung your new nickname on you; watch, the captain and everyone else will be calling you 'Marty' too. You finish the typing, I'll fill the Xerox machine with fresh paper, hurry now that coffee will only give us a few minutes. After that you can shove off for the day. I'll stick around here in case the boss has anything else for us, but this afternoon I'm hitting the beach too, as soon as I can get ahold of my friends on *Porter* and *Monty*. You heard the places to stay away from ashore so be careful but have a great liberty day. I'll see you in the morning right here at 0700. There won't be a department head meeting but there will still be mail to handle."

She had a thought, "Hey Marty I just thought of something; would you like to meet some of the guys on *Monty?* If you wanna hang around until after I check with the boss I'll take you aboard and introduce you to some really great guys! See they don't have any women in the crew so they are starving for feminine company. But once you make friends with them you've got it made they're really a tight-knit group."

"Are you sure we can go aboard Sam? Isn't that whole submarine thing like top secret and everything?"

"Don't worry Marty;" she laughed. "Just stick with me and do what I do!"

They took the typed sheets back to the captain's mess and passed them out. Wilson stood next to the admiral and said, "Commander Cushman and Commander Gavin we'll take copies down to your XOs and command master chiefs, so you can enjoy your lunch here with the Captain."

They smiled and thanked her and the captain made his thumbs up sign so Wilson knew it would be okay to shove off. She turned toward the door and remembered something, turning back to address the assistant attaché, "Sir I'm sure all the shops are nice, but are there any that the embassy staff and families frequent for Persian rugs or other gift items?"

It was such a great question that it would take a special effort to answer it. The embassy man said he would send a list that afternoon, after he spoke with some of the embassy wives. Wilson smiled and thanked him, it was too bad that the embassy hadn't sent a woman briefer too. A woman would have had that information right at the tip of her tongue. She was sure now that the Captain's assessment of the State Department and their efforts was spot on. At least the Algerian officials had brought along a list of places *not* to go.

The admiral left then, on his way back to the flag spaces. Wilson knew he was feeling good because he went off humming "*I am the monarch of the seas…*".

The captain shooed his yeomen off after the meeting and Wilson led the way to *Montpelier*. They were welcomed aboard by the XO and the COB who quickly passed out the port information and briefed their liberty party. Wilson introduced Fernandez to her friends in the crew. The women had to take a rain check on lunch with them because they had to hurry to *Porter* and hand over the briefing sheets to their destroyer friends, but they ran into Manckowicz who hugged Wilson and told her he had the duty that day. If they stayed aboard they could join him and Dorothy for lunch in the crew's mess, she would be joining him as soon as she finished some outgoing letters for her captain.

Wilson giggled, "Ted I got a letter from Ron just the other day, he said to tell you hello and he wishes you were there with him. He's playing football for the NAPS team and he says they could really use a good pulling guard! Hey if you and Dorothy want to go with me on liberty tomorrow I was planning on doing some shopping. The embassy is supposed to be sending us the names of the shops the staff goes to all the time, I'm looking for a pretty rug for my mom and one of those funny hats with a tassel on it for Daddy. Marty is coming with me and if Billy Bates isn't busy he's coming too. It'll be fun Ted, we'll find a nice French restaurant, you know how Dorothy loves exotic foods!"

If anything could inspire Manckowicz to go adventuring it was the promise of food. The mere notion of rich creamy sauces, meats dripping with savory juices and tasty desserts was enough to coax her large friend into the liberty party. He was far from being a gourmand but he knew what he liked, and lots of it!

"Okay Sam you've won me over. I'll talk to Dorothy and we'll meet you wherever and whenever you say." He could taste their lunch already.

The women left then to hurry across to *Porter,* where the XO and command master chief thanked them for the materials and quickly set up a crew briefing. Wilson found a few of her *Porter* friends and introduced her protégée to her girlfriend; "Dorothy this is Marty Fernandez she's new but I set it up so that she'll be my relief when I'm detached back in Norfolk. She's a great shipmate already."

Stanfield knew that if Sam rated her that highly she must be pretty special indeed, "Hi Marty, I'm Dorothy and I'm engaged to

Sam's old next door neighbor Ted."

Fernandez giggled, "Is he the giant blonde guy on *Montpelier* with the wonderful grin and the puppy dog eyes?"

Dorothy smiled knowingly, Fernandez had described him to a T, "Yes that's my handsome darling Teddy!"

Wilson was laughing now, "Dorothy we just saw Ted on *Montpelier* and he's anxious for you to join him there. But tomorrow I'd like to do some sightseeing and shopping and it would be fun to go with you and Ted, I'll bring Billy and Judy with me, Marty's coming too. This afternoon she and I are going to reconnoiter a little and see if my French lessons have any value!"

As they walked back to their berthing compartment to change into their dress whites Fernandez made her observation, "Sam this whole morning I've watched you, there isn't anybody who doesn't know who you are, even on the other ships. You're the most popular person I know!"

Wilson laughed. "Marty I know the *Monty* guys because I was underway with them for two days and I know the *Porter* guys because I've stayed onboard and I was marooned with five of them for a few days. You'll be in the same position as me in a few weeks. Just relax and smile a lot, I know you can handle it."

CHAPTER 4
SIGHTSEEING WITH MUSTAFA

THEIR AFTERNOON OF SIGHTSEEING BEGAN with a short walk up the Rue de Beauvais, past the seaport area, to a taxi stand where they flagged a dusty cab. The Citroen took them through the center of the old city while Mustafa, their mustachioed, quasi bi-lingual driver, pointed out the sights and made suggestions for their follow-on visit the next day with their friends. He pointed out shops on the Rue Didouche Mourad which all appeared to be owned and operated by various brothers, cousins or nephews and he even showed them a restaurant that les Mademoiselles would surely find to be to their "most exqueezeet taste and likingness".

    Wilson laughed and whispered to Fernandez that their guide looked a bit like one of the big Yorkshire boars that lived on a farm near hers back in Iowa, except for his voluminous mustache which stuck out from beneath his nose like a pair of shaggy gray bird wings. Fernandez began laughing and almost missed the group of sailors sauntering along the avenue, whistling at every female in sight and obviously in love with themselves. They wore the same white color as their American allies, but they sported white shorts and bare legs, jumpers with squared off necklines and silly white hats with blue bands around their bases and red pom poms at their tops. Wilson thought they looked a bit like the sailors' costumes she'd had made for her "Tars" but they were decidedly different, these were uniforms of French sailors from the two warships they had seen tied up alongside the quay wall.

Wilson pointed to them as they rattled past, "Marty look at those clowns, do they really think they can make a pickup on the street in those ridiculous-looking sailor 'costumes'? Look at those silly 'Donald Duck' hats with the ridiculous red puff balls on top!"

Fernandez giggled, "Sam they look so different! Our uniforms are similar; all white, except for our neckerchiefs. They have those bib-looking things I wonder if it's because they are messy eaters! Maybe they'll think our uniforms look silly."

Wilson nodded laughingly, "I wonder if our guys would like a pair of white shorts in this heat? At least we women get to wear skirts. You know Marty, we're going to run into some of these French guys around town so we'd better get used to being whistled at and figure out the best way to react. Maybe we should whistle right back at them!"

Their driver cringed when he heard Wilson's remark, "Mademoiselle the French, they are peegs it was only a few years ago that the FLN was able to free us from the subjugation of their rule. Believe me there is no love between them and us Algerians. The French treated us as ahhneemals they wanted to starve us out so they could have the best land and these gens de mer, ces marins, ils continuent à revenir en nous rappelant du passé triste. C'est très triste."

Wilson got the gist of what he was saying, "Marty he's saying that when the French sailors come back here it reminds them of the past. He says it is so sad. I'm going to try some of the French I've picked up."

"Je suis désolé, Monsieur, mais on ne peut pas attribuer la responsabilité des erreurs du passé à ces jeunes hommes. Vous devez les pardonner."

Fernandez's eyes grew as big as teacups, "Sam that was wonderful! What did you say to him?"

Wilson giggled, "Well I was trying to say that those sailors aren't to blame for the mistakes of the past and he should cut them some slack but maybe I asked him to take us to the coconut market.

We'll see!"

Their driver smiled then, "Mademoiselle, vous êtes aussi gentile que belle."

Wilson was pretty sure he'd said she was both kind and beautiful and she decided to change the subject. "S'il vous plaît, Monsieur, pourriez-vous nous emmener à la Kasbah et à un bon café?" Then she turned to her friend, "I hope he takes us to a nice coffee shop in the Kasbah and not to the town dump!"

The taxi turned east and rumbled up Chemin Cheickh Bashir Ibrahimi El-Biar Street and they saw the American flags on the front façade outside the US Embassy. Wilson wondered if there was a facility inside where they might be able to change dollars to dinars and she remembered that the assistant attaché still owed them the list of shops frequented by the embassy staff. Perhaps they could stop and find out where that stood. She looked at the driver's photo-license card clipped to the underside of the right sun visor. It read: MADJER, MUSTAFA, and she tried her best, "S'il vous plaît Monsieur Madjer, pourriez-vous arrêter ici pour un moment?"

The driver pulled to the side of the street, "Bien sûr mademoiselle. Je vous attendre ici."

Wilson slid across the seat and opened the rear door motioning for Fernandez to follow her. "Merci Monsieur. Nous revenons tout de suit." She turned to her companion, "I told him we'd be quick."

The US Marine sentry outside the door admitted the two women sailors after they showed their ID cards. He also indicated that there was a window in a side hallway where they could change some money. Wilson thanked him with a smile. Inside the foyer, a table held a telephone for in-house use along with a listing of embassy personnel and their numbers. Wilson dialed the assistant attaché who had briefed them that morning. It was answered after the second ring. "Hello, James Parker."

Wilson hoped he'd had a chance to get the information she was looking for. "Hello Mr. Parker, it's Petty Officer Wilson from *USS Eisenhower*, I stopped by to pick up that list of shops we talked about this morning at the arrival briefing. I'm waiting downstairs in the vestibule if you have it ready."

She turned to Fernandez and quipped, "Now we'll see how efficient the State Department is."

They had time to change some dollars into dinars at the barred security window and Wilson showed Fernandez her trick of folding the bills and sticking them into her skirt pocket. It was much safer than using a purse for her cash. A black navy purse was a tempting target for a snatcher, and they had already learned that there were plenty of those around Algiers.

The official did have a list ready, and he came down the stairs to greet them. "Are you Miss Wilson?"

She smiled, "Actually Sir it's Petty Officer Wilson, but if you call me Sam or even 'Sailor' it will do. This is Seaman Marty Fernandez, she's in charge of making sure that all of the six thousand people on *Ike* and the five hundred other people on *Porter* and *Montpelier* have this information. I'm sure that the shops involved will thank you for this input."

The list included the names of the shops, their addresses and the items that the embassy wives recommended as bargains. There was even a list of restaurants with little asterisks by each; one meant "okay" four stood for "outstanding".

The official laughed and pointed out the French restaurant he and his wife liked the most and also showed them the one that had the to-die-for Algerian seafood. He pointed his finger at what his wife would swear was the best Persian rug shop in all of North Africa and even recommended a shop where Wilson could find an authentic fez and a Bedouin's tribal head scarf.

Wilson thanked him effusively and asked if he would be coming back out to *Ike* with his wife for dinner during their round of entertainment. He told her that his wife was very excited about it and was probably out right then trying on new dresses suitable for their dinner aboard ship. Wilson laughed, "I hope your wife doesn't buy anything too fancy or too impractical, she will have to climb ladders just to get aboard and sometimes that can be a problem in a skirt. The really high heels can be a problem too, but if you give her your arm it shouldn't be dangerous. If you get to the ship a little before dinner time and you'd like a tour around, just let us know and we'd be happy to show you and your wife around, even the others if they're interested, just ask for Sam or Marty."

He grinned, "Well thank you Sam, I'm sure my wife would love to have you show us around, *Eisenhower* is quite a huge vessel. Are you the designated tour guide or are you a volunteer?"

Fernandez giggled, "Mr. Parker, Sam is the person you should always ask for; she knows everyone and she can get anything done. If you're with her you'll get to see it all."

Wilson laughed, "Marty is taking over for me when I leave the ship after we get back to Norfolk Sir. She's getting her feet wet right now aboard, but believe me she can more than hold her own with anything that has to do with *Ike*. Well, we have a driver waiting outside, we'd better go now we're headed to the Kasbah for a look around and a cup of coffee. We're hoping to see you again soon and thank your wife for me please." She held up the sheet he'd provided and the two women sailors turned and left him by the phone table.

Outside, Wilson gave the Marine sentry a big smile and said, "Thank you Corporal, they should let you stand your post in the shade. It must be ninety five out here. Hey if you get a chance come on out and we'll give you a good meal on *Ike*. Bring the rest of your guy's too, just tell the quarterdeck watch you're looking for Marty Fernandez or Sam Wilson."

He smiled and nodded as they descended the stairs and walked to the waiting taxi. Wilson opened the door and slid across the back seat, letting Fernandez get in before she instructed their driver. "Je vous remercie Monsieur, nous sommes prêts à continuer notre aventure maintenant. On à la Kasbah!"

The driver laughed, cranked up the temperamental engine and they lurched off up the broad street in pursuit of a coffee shop. He deposited them at one that he said was a favorite of European tourists and offered to wait for them. "Mademoiselle s'il vous le désirez je vais rester ici et attendre pour vous."

Wilson gave him her most fetching smile, "Très bien, Monsieur, vous êtes très aimable."

The women got out of the cab and entered the building, the ancient wooden doorway led to a long narrow room with a center passageway and low-beamed ceilings. Small round-topped tables hugged the walls and a welcoming waiter showed them to one near the center and placed small menus by each of the two chairs. Wilson sat with her back to the door and spied the bar and kitchen area at the back of the room. She looked up at the waiter and smiled, "Nous pouvons avoir deux cafés s'il vous plaît?"

"Oui bien sûr Mademoiselle." He hurried off to bring them their coffees.

They were stirring in cream and sugar when the door opened and the little group of French sailors entered behind them. Fernandez was surprised and she didn't know what to say, "Sam don't look now, but a bunch of those French guys just walked in."

There were six of them, and they took the tables on either side of the two American women, grabbing extra chairs to accommodate themselves. Within moments the attempt to pick them up began, as one of the group tried out his limited English. "Hey girls, want to have some dreenks weeth us?"

Wilson shot a mirthful glance at Fernandez, "If we say no they'll probably think we're lesbians Marty, and if we say yes they'll think we're easy."

The French petty officer understood most of what he'd heard and began to share his hopeful thoughts with his shipmates when Wilson interrupted, "Bonjour mes amis et alliés, nous sommes américains marins de femmes de *l'USS Eisenhower*. Je suis Sam et cela mon ami Marty. Nous sommes seulement ici pour prendre un café et ensuite nous devons revenir sur notre navire. Quel est votre bateau?"

Taken by surprise the men all began yammering away at once and Wilson smilingly held up her hand, "S'il vous plaît un à la fois!

Je n'ai que deux oreilles et mon Français est nouvellement apprise!"

When the Frenchmen stopped laughing and calmed down they explained that they were from the big destroyer *Duquesne*, the ship they'd seen with the wide boxy stern. Over the next half hour they traded stories of storms at sea, joint US-French exercises in the Mediterranean, and liberty hijinks in Marseilles, their home port. They invited them to visit *Duquesne* and have lunch or dinner with them aboard boasting that they had some very excellent French wine that they were privileged to have with their meals. They even clamored to swap hats with the two pretty women sailors.

Wilson laughed and asked for a rain check, "Merci pour l'invitation, mes amis, mais si nous pouvons attendre quelques jours? Nous sommes tous deux très occupé ce soir et demain. Peut-être, nous avons pu visiter le vendredi pour le déjeuner."

She turned to her protégée, "Marty we're on for lunch aboard on Friday."

They found their driver outside in deep conversation with several other drivers but he quickly broke off discussion in favor of returning the two "belle Ahhmareicains" to the waterfront. He even volunteered his services as principal driver "chauffer de taxi principal" for the duration of their stay. Any of *Ike's* sailors would be treated by him with the utmost care and respect as only "la belle et sage femme marin" would expect and demand.

Wilson laughed. "Marty I think our friend wants to be the official taxi driver for the ship. I don't think that can be bad but we'll have to check and we'll leave word with the shore patrol that Monsieur Madjer is an excellent driver and that he can be counted on to charge the lowest bargain rates for every *Ike* sailor."

CHAPTER 5
A CRITICAL ERROR

NO ONE COULD HAVE PREDICTED the fire. It started in the temporary junction box that *Ike's* EMs had set up on the weather deck to allow power from their switchboard down through the big power cables to *Monty* via her engine room hatch. The first sign of trouble had been the indication of an increasing ground on *Monty's* shore power bus. And then, before the SMAW could do anything about it, *Ike's* switchboard operators had tripped out the offending condition leaving *Montpelier* on battery power alone. The SMAW got the word out quickly and the duty officer ordered the ship rigged for reduced electrical and prepared to snorkel. With their diesel on the line they would be able to handle all their shipboard loads, at least until the ground was corrected and power from *Ike* was restored.

It only took a few minutes to complete the snorkeling lineup. The diesel was soon up to speed and carrying the ship's loads, and the crew and their guests could get back to watching the evening movie in the crew's mess. Wilson and Stanfield shared a table near the back with Manckowicz, Bates and Obenauf. Fernandez, Carbury and Turner had joined them too and were enjoying their first exposure to the camaraderie of the submarine force. Tonight's flick had been hyped by the studio's advertising men for months before it's release and the mere fact that *Montpelier* had it aboard, was testimony that the navy MPX system was very efficient at getting new releases to the fleet. Everyone was keyed up to watch this blockbuster, if only *Gandhi* was really as good as all the film critics had said it was. Ben Kingsley was the odds-on favorite to take home Oscar gold for his portrayal of the famous martyr who had striven so hard for India's independence.

TM3 Lupo had just threaded the first of the epic's four reels into the projector and was ready to roll it when the general alarm began sounding; the loud BONG, BONG, BONGING certainly got everyone's attention.

A leaky line in the fuel system of one of *Ike's* A6 tankers, parked at the edge of the flight deck well astern, had allowed the viscous fluid to pool under the fuselage. It went undetected by the roving fire and safety watch because a "huffer"—one of the heavy, portable power units they used to start the jet's engines—parked between planes, hid the pool. A miniscule list, owing to the forces of the currents working on *Ike's* gigantic hull at anchor, allowed the pooled jet fuel to drip from the edge of the flight deck and run down the bulkhead, to reform in a corner of the weather deck, just under the temporary junction box where *Monty's* power cables coupled the two ships together electrically. Sparked by the electrical problem, the pool caught fire and began to blaze, emitting dense black smoke. It would eventually burn itself out, but not before it cooked off the rounds in the ready storage lockers next to one of *Ike's* BPDMS mounts. It wouldn't be very healthy for the planes parked nearby either. The cascading sequence of events might have been disastrous.

Monty's duty officer was alerted by the topside watch's alarming report of flame and smoke coming from *Ike's* weather deck just above *Monty's* engine room trunk. He picked up the phone in control to call and warn *Ike's* quarterdeck and rang the general alarm at the same time. When the quarterdeck relayed the need for help in fighting the fire he called away the duty section, executing the ASSIST SHIP BILL to provide fire-fighting support to the flagship. All thought of watching the flick went out the window as the crew down in the crew's mess hurried to break out the equipment *Monty* would need to help combat the fire.

The CDO's call to inform Captain Christensen of the problem came just after Admiral Townsend, his captains and the lucky officers chosen to accompany them to the formal dinner in the embassy had put down their cocktail glasses and assembled at the dinner table. Christensen made his apologies and raced for the door. A hastily hailed taxi hustled him and his officers to the pier where his gig was standing by. Certainly his crew could handle a fire aboard, but his ship was his ship, he wanted to be there if anything was amiss. The ultimate responsibility for any problem and it's solution was his. The minutes spent in that taxi, out of communication with the ship and not knowing what was happening, were the most frustrating in his career.

One *Montpelier* team, consisting of the six visiting women sailors in their dungarees sprang into action. They assembled and dragged a hose up the bridge trunk. From there they could play a stream of water from the highest point on the sail, up a dozen and back perhaps forty feet, onto the blaze. Manckowicz donned an OBA and led Bates and a few others forming their second hose team up the gangway toward the weather deck. They would combat the fire from close up, with a fog nozzle. It took every length of fire hose on the boat, coupled together, to allow the fire teams to climb into position for the attempt to battle the blaze.

When Manckowicz reported READY TO PRESSURIZE via the phonetalker, the duty chief pressurized the trim system header from the air-loaded forward trim tank. The water, helped along by the 700 psi service air, immediately found it's way via the hoses out of the boat and *Monty's* fire parties were in business. The combination of the two streams was exactly what it took to win the day. *Ike's* fire parties, approaching the blaze from the flight deck, had been held back by the thick and worsening back smoke. The water from *Monty's* trim header was the key to *Ike's* salvation. Within minutes the blaze was knocked down and then overhauled. Within a few more, the men in *Ike's* weapons department could access the area and were able to verify that the rounds in their ready lockers were unharmed.

Ike's CDO put in a call to the embassy to report that the fire had been overhauled with the help of their able nest mates and they were working on restoring electrical power to them as well. Captain Christensen had just arrived at the pier and was about to jump aboard the gig when the shore patrol officer raced out from his little office-shack and passed the word that the CDO had just reported that the fire had been overhauled, the ordnance was unharmed, and everyone was safe.

By the time they had secured from the casualty, drained and re-stowed the fire hoses, and Manckowicz and Bates disposed of their expended OBA canisters, it was too late to run the flick they had started watching. Ben Kingsley would have to wait until another day. The duty chief suggested they show something shorter, something that wouldn't interfere with mid-rats. A quick poll of the movie-goers resulted in a clear winner. They would rerun a crew favorite; *Grease,* the high energy, high octane, musical comedy that was guaranteed to make them all feel good.

During the wait while one of the men ran off to find the movie, Fernandez sprang the news that Wilson was directing *Ike's* upcoming comic opera. Bates took a bow as she ticked off the names of the players in her cast. Manckowicz was effusive in his praise and at the same time wished that he could transfer to *Ike* for at least long enough to be part of the show. It sounded like a lot of fun.

Wilson told them that she'd finally solved the one remaining costume problem which was the lack of colorful dresses for the First Lord's sisters, his cousins and his aunts. The flag secretary had found some old parachutes among the air squadrons and had them donated for the show. The silk would be dyed and sewn into bright, colorful, and stylish circa 1880s dresses by the volunteer seamstresses in their tailor shop. All it had taken was the flag sec's phoned assurance that "Sam needs the 'chutes". They had been delivered to the tailor shop within the hour.

When they were ready to roll the first reel of *Grease* the duty chief assured their visitors that they would show *Gandhi* another evening.

Christensen was piped aboard just as his EMs were ready to restore temporary power to *Monty*. A quick briefing from the men in damage control central was all he needed. A personal tour of the fire scene and a quick wash up with his CDO revealed to him the need to say a few words of thanks to the duty section aboard *Monty*.

When the topside watch announced DWIGHT D EISENHOWER ARRIVING the duty officer raced topside to greet him. He indicated that they were just securing their diesel because temporary power had just been restored. The only glitch in the whole evening had been the interruption of the crew's movie when the fire parties were called away to help *Ike*. Christensen thanked him for the help *Monty* had provided, in so timely a manner. It was quite possibly the first time in navy history that a US submarine had put out a fire on a US carrier. If it was okay with the duty officer he'd like to personally convey his thanks to the men in *Monty's* duty section.

The duty officer shot him a grin, "Sure thing Captain but that isn't quite accurate, it's men in the duty section alright, but it also was some women sailors that you may know. They manned the hose up on the sail. Follow me Sir, I know they'd all like to hear from you!"

He followed the young lieutenant down the hatch and they joined the group in the crew's mess just as the "Pink Lady slumber party scene" began. There was a burst of laughter as the two officers arrived and stood at the doorway taking in the scene. Christensen recognized one of those laughs and he wasn't a bit surprised. His favorite woman sailor had somehow found her way into the center of the action again. In the flickering light of the projector he could see that there were other women there in the darkness with her, seated together at an outboard table. There must be four or five of them, good shipmates all. It wouldn't do to interrupt them at their fun. He tapped the lieutenant on the shoulder and gestured for him to come away with him. When they got to the upper level ops compartment he asked the lieutenant to send him a list of the sailors who had been involved in putting out the fire, including all hands in *Monty's* duty section. He would put his gratitude into writing in the morning. The laughing girl on *Monty's* mess decks would have to help him again, her liberty status notwithstanding.

"Lieutenant it's okay, I don't want to throw a wrench into their spokes. That's *Grease* they're watching isn't it?"

"Yes Sir, they started with *Gandhi* but the fire intervened, we'll probably run that tomorrow night."

"Great, thank you for everything and let me get out of your hair. I wonder if I can get back to the embassy by the time they roll out the sherbet course. No need to take me topside Lieutenant, have a good watch."

He persuaded the young topside watch to refrain from announcing his departure, he would leave quickly and quietly, sure that his command was safe and his sailors secure. With any luck at all he could rejoin the revelers at the embassy in time to have dessert.

His jovial reappearance in the dining room reassured the admiral, his officers and their embassy hosts. A bit of gray paint was all that would be necessary to erase any evidence of the fire. He thanked Commander Cushman for his command's rapid and effective help in overhauling the blaze and apologized for interrupting their crew's movie earlier in the evening. "I understand they had just begun watching *Gandhi* when it happened, and because of the delay for the fire it's too long a movie for tonight, they'll see it another night. I apologize for delaying your crew's entertainment."

The ambassador's wife was intrigued, *"Gandhi!* Captain I've read it's probably a 'Best Picture' *shoo in!* We're always so far behind the rest of the world here getting any new releases. Can we work something out for another night?"

Commander Cushman nodded smilingly, and without another word the die was cast, and the stage set … for disaster.

CHAPTER 6
LE JARDIN D' ESSAI

WILSON SURELY WASN'T SURPRISED, THE captain had just handed her the list of sailors he wanted mentioned by name for their outstanding help in his letter to *Montpelier*. He had circled each of her women shipmates' names in red and added a notation in red too. It read: "Make up OPNAV Form1650s and get these women medals." He had circled her name in black and written: "MSM for this one." Then he shooed her off to her office. She thought she could bang out the letter in very short order but the awards paperwork would take her most of the morning.

"Aye, aye Captain, I'll have the letter ready in a few minutes but can I wait on the awards recommendations 'til tomorrow? I was going to go ashore and do some shopping today, I can postpone it if you need them right away though Sir."

He chuckled, "No Sam, go ahead and do your shopping but first, tell me how you got involved with that fire last night. I saw you sitting on the mess decks afterward with those other women but I didn't want to break in on your evening."

She giggled, "I was visiting Petty Officer Manckowicz Captain. Billy Bates, Judy Obenauf and I went to say hello and I took my other friends, Marty Fernandez, Stef Turner, and Pam Carbury along so they could see what it's like aboard a sub. Dorothy was already there having supper with Ted. We stayed to watch their movie and when the general alarm rang it was just a natural thing to do. I took the other girls and we formed our own fire team. Dorothy knew where the hose was and I had some experience with their bridge and we just ran the hose up the trunk and supported the hose team that Ted Manckowicz led up the accommodation ladder. Billy Bates was the first to volunteer to go along with him. He should get a medal if *anyone* does Captain."

"Thank you Sam I missed it. Put him on the list too please, did I miss anyone else?"

"Your letter to *Montpelier* is meant for her CO to use for medals for his own guys, right Sir?"

"Exactly Sam."

"Then you need to write a letter to *Porter* too Captain. Dorothy Stanfield was right there beside me on that nozzle."

Christensen shrugged, "You're right again Sam, for a minute there I forgot she's a *Porter* sailor, I'm so used to seeing her with those sub driver guys. Oh and while you're on the letters I need words in them like: 'without regard for their personal safety in the face of a hazardous fire that involved dangerous explosive ordnance stored adjacent to it,' those folks went 'over and above the call' when they rushed that fire."

Wilson hurried to her office and fired up the mag card machine, she had pre-stored all the navy standard subject indicator codes so it was a minor matter to pull up the appropriate administrivia that went at the top of every bit of navy correspondence, that part was trivial. She was able to concentrate on the actual wording of the letters and used up almost all of the superlative adjectives she could think of describing the actions of *Monty's* people and then *Porter's* favorite daughter in their prompt and effective assistance to *Eisenhower*. She found that the words came easily because she had been in the middle of the incident too. She'd had a bird's eye view of the men as they rushed up that accommodation ladder, not caring that all those explosives could go up like a white-hot Roman candle. The captain was right, this was certainly a case of "over and above the call of duty". It was a case of brave men doing *everything they could* to save their brothers on *Ike*. Thank goodness *Monty's* topside watch had spotted the blaze early enough so they could make a difference.

Wilson finished the draft letters and took them back to the captain's cabin, "I've got the letters ready Captain."

"C'mon in Sam let's see what you've come up with."

She stepped inside and walked to his desk, "Here they are Boss."

He took them from her and scanned the one to *Montpelier* first. She had specifically called out every one of the sailors she was sure had fought the fire and included the duty chief and duty officer in a separate paragraph extolling their leadership during the emergency. She'd even included a separate paragraph praising the sailors on watch, or who in other ways, had supported the men and women in the fire teams. She'd written it just perfectly; it was an action-filled narrative, not a dispassionate, somber, ho-hum, third person account like so many reports seemed to be. They had their place too of course, but not in describing the courageous actions of good sailors and shipmates who had risked their lives for his ship.

"Thank you Sam this is just what I wanted," he picked up his pen and signed it without changing a thing. "Is the one to *Porter* as good?"

"Well it's different Captain there was only my friend Dorothy to write about but I think it may be even better than the first one."

When he looked it over he agreed with her and signed it. Then he handed it back to her laughing, "Sam I'll see you tomorrow, try not to get involved in any big emergencies ashore, okay? I'm looking forward to seeing your 1650's, let me see who you think walks on water!"

She giggled, "Captain I'm meeting those brave women and a couple of those brave men and we're going to check out the shops where the bargains are. Oh, I have an invitation to have lunch on that French ship, the *Duquesne*. Don't worry though Captain I'll have the 1650s ready before I go ashore tomorrow."

Christensen chuckled, "How'd you wrangle a lunch on *Duques-*

ne Sam?"

She laughed, "I went ashore with Marty yesterday and we went to a coffee shop. A bunch of French sailors came in and tried to pick us up. They didn't know that I can speak just a little bit of French so I was able to impress them I think. Know what Captain? They have wine with their meals! Maybe they know a better way of doing crew morale than we do!"

He grimaced, "Maybe so Sam, but I think you'll see a real difference in how the French keep their ships up in comparison to how we do it. After your visit come and let's compare notes I'll bet you're surprised by the difference. Now go ahead and get out of here, have a good time with your friends ashore."

"Aye, aye Captain," she chirped. "Can I pick up anything for you ashore Sir?"

He laughed, "No thank you Sam but let me know what you think of the rugs when you get back."

"Yes Sir." She waved gaily as she opened his door and left the room.

She met Bates and Obenauf on the quarterdeck and they waited for Manckowicz and Stanfield to join them. They were on their way down the boarding ladder to catch the next launch ashore when Fernandez and Turner caught up with them, their work for the day completed.

The liberty launch was only half filled when the cox'n signaled to their bowhook to take in the line and he revved the engine to leave the boom behind. Shifting the rudder and clutching the engine to go ahead, they were soon on their way toward a new adventure in this ancient Berber port city with modern buildings going up, all around the old part of the town, the result of plenty of French reinvestment. Wilson remembered that this new nation had still been an actual French colony as late as 1962, only twenty-odd years before. The brochures their boarding officer had given them listed the Presidential Palace as having once been the seat of the Governor General. He had apparently had to find a new job after the fighting between the

French Foreign Legion and the FLN rebels.

She could see that there was some activity aboard the smaller of the two French navy ships. They were depressing the muzzle on her forward gun mount. She thought perhaps it meant they were performing PMs, like the ones Ron had told her about on *Porter* when they exercised the mount to make sure it was shipshape and ready at any moment for use. She could see that there were a number of their battle group sailors too, down by the landing and waiting for the liberty launch to catch a ride back to the ships. Some of them were laden with goods they had bought while ashore. There was a chief with a huge wooden and metal bird cage. Wilson wondered where he was going to store it until they returned to the states in November.

When the launch was alongside the landing, the Cox'n shifted to reverse and idled in gently against the float at the quay wall. The bowhook made them fast and the mixed group of sailors eagerly disembarked. Bates led them up the few steps from the float to the street level and Wilson could see what their next problem would be. A band of young boys, some tiny and hardly out of kindergarten, some larger who appeared to be of high school age, were there between the pier and the street, engaging in their trade. They were beggar boys and they yammered away, pleading with the American sailors for coins, for candy and chewing gum or for any of the parts of their uniforms they could get. Wilson was wise to them, not only were they beggars, they were also accomplished thieves. They had been sent out by the 'prince of thieves' to bring back valuables. Wallets, purses, cameras, anything that could be taken would be sold later in the thieves market, the back alley shops in the old city. Money and cigarettes were especially prized.

Wilson knew it wouldn't be wise to fight with them, it would be far easier if she could convince the children to leave them alone for now, "Let me try something." She held out her arms to them, "Alors, les petits, venes render visite après qu'on ait fait les courses. Nous reviendrons. Venez m'embrasser pour me porter chance."

There was a surge as the urchins crowded around the tall pretty sailor and she stooped, to hug and kiss the smallest of them while her friends joined in with her, hugging the poor children in their ragged clothes. Wilson explained that she had told the kids not to bother them until after they returned from shopping.

Then she put the children to work, "Les enfants, s'il vous plaît, vous pouvez m'aider à trouver le taxi de Monsieur Madjer." She ruffled the smallest boy's unruly hair as he pointed her toward the taxi stand and the Sultan of the taxi drivers.

"C'mon everyone I hope we can all fit in Mustafa's cab, Marty and I rode with him yesterday when we came ashore to get the lay of the land. Actually if we can't all fit in he'll probably have a friend who can help."

The smiling cab driver welcomed her, "Bonjour, la belle, où puis-je vous emmener ce matin?"

She laughed merrily, "Bonjour Monsieur, pourriez-vous nous emmener au Jardin d'Essai s'il vous plaît?" She turned to Bates and Manckowicz, "The guidebook says it's stunningly beautiful and the briefing officer said they have food stands and little shops all over the gardens so Ted there will be something you'll like, I'm sure of it!"

Manckowicz wasn't hungry just yet, it was only a couple of hours since breakfast, but with the sun high in the sky and the temperature already in the high 80s he knew it would be time for a cold beer very soon. Stanfield slid into the back seat of the taxi and pulled her big submariner in after her. She would make it easier to load the back seat, and climbed up onto her fiancé's lap, content to cuddle him. She loved to sit on his lap and tickle him behind the ear. Wilson was able to squeeze in with her two other women friends, but Bates and Obenauf would have to ride in the next cab. Fortunately, Mustafa's nephew had an identical Citroen and was more than glad to follow his uncle's lead. The friends and shipmates watched the buildings go by as the taxis negotiated the Rue Tancrede and deposited them at the gate to the park-like gardens. Their mustachioed driver would take no fare, insisting instead that he would drive to the other end of the gorgeous grounds and await them there. He would then transport them to the shops that Wilson had asked him about. He was keen to be of service to the white-uniformed men and women from the ships anchored majestically in the outer harbor.

The flowers and trees in the lush garden setting were as delightful as any that they had ever seen. Manckowicz picked out half a dozen different varieties of palm tree and there were countless flowers of every shade imaginable. It was obvious that there must be a legion of gardeners who maintained the charming place. The fragrances of the flowers clashed with the aromas of the food and snack vendors that lined the pathways. Stanfield bought a little sack of fat, delicious dates and passed them around for her friends to try. Manckowicz thought they were almost as good as the blood oranges he had grown so fond of when *Montpelier* had her Israeli port visit two months ago.

Wilson bought some pastries that reminded them all of the souvlaki they had all loved so much during their Greek port visit. Bates told them he thought that they were eating their way through all the different cultures in the Mediterranean. They had yet to find a local delicacy that tasted badly. Manckowicz believed that they were probably very lucky because the weather had been so wonderful for most of their Med cruise. Except for a brief time in late March, there had been no big storms and they'd reaped the benefit of that. The battle group that would be arriving to relieve them would have the winter months to look forward to and their siroccos blowing out of North Africa. While nowhere near as cold and stormy as the North Atlantic, the Mediterranean could still throw a nasty squall or two at navy ships in the winter time.

Wilson assembled all her friends and got one of the pastry vendors to take their photographs with the beautiful white walls of the garden's gazebo and fountains in the background. She would have her friends in the ship's photo lab make copies so they could each have one and she knew her fiancé and her parents would love to get one too. They exited the palatial gardens at the opposite end and as promised their favorite driver was there to take them on their shopping trip.

They browsed the rugs in the first shop and Wilson found a handsome deep-blue Bokhara rug with golden medallions woven into it. She thought it would look lovely inside the front doorway of her parent's home. The shopkeeper only spoke Arabic and Berber so Wilson wasn't able to bargain with him. Fernandez was helpful, "Sam why don't I go bring Mr. Madjer in and he can translate for you?"

"Great idea Marty!"

The demonstrative driver was only too happy to assist and the merchant *was* after all, a distant relative of his, and after three rounds of offer and counter-offer he managed to drive the price for the handsome rug down to the merchant's rock bottom rate. *But* Wilson had to promise to tell *all* her friends on the huge gray warship that it had come from Achmed's rug shop on Avenue Franklin Roosevelt. When she realized that she was paying a tenth what the rug had been initially advertised for, she knew it was indeed a bargain. Similar rugs went for over fifty dollars per square foot, her four by six rug was probably worth over a thousand dollars. She paid less than a hundred.

The others bought things from the rug man too, afterward they went to a shop where Wilson was able to buy her father a scarlet fez with a gold tassel and she bought a pair of Bedouin head scarves, one for her mother and one for herself. Her friends made excellent bargain purchases too and then Wilson asked Monsieur Madjer to take them to Le Normand on the Rue Tancrede, according to their embassy man it supposedly served the best French food in the whole city.

They were greeted and seated quickly, their early evening arrival was in the crease between the late afternoon diners and the first of the evening's gourmands. They were shown to a large table in an alcove where they could enjoy the ambiance but still have the private feel of an intimate gathering of friends. Two waiters were assigned to their table and Stanfield would be able to pick the dishes she thought her brave and wonderful fiancé would enjoy the most. Manckowicz approved of every dish that she picked out for them and showed his appreciation with his trademark lopsided grin.

Wilson was seated at the foot of the table with her friends arrayed on either side, she gave them a smile and began describing her morning's work. "My boss gave me a task this morning and I thought I'd tell you a bit about it. Because of the fire last night I had to write letters to *Montpelier* and to *Porter* thanking the men and women involved in putting it out. He is recommending medals for the people who helped *Ike* last night. Tomorrow morning I have to write up a bunch of medal recommendations for the *Ike* personnel that helped. The captain thinks that everyone involved was heroic."

Manckowicz was aghast, "Sam I don't know why he'd think we were heroic, I just didn't want whatever was on fire up there on that weather deck to fall down on top of the boat!"

Wilson joined the others in laughing at the big blonde sailor's thought. Only Ted could try to brush off a heroic act by finding some silly way to side track the conversation. She remembered how he'd tried to put all the credit for saving those young people in Israel on his beloved Dorothy, two months ago during *Monty's* port visit in Ashdod. But the Prime Minister of Israel had been overcome with joy because of Ted's brave actions. He'd disregarded his own safety and gotten the young people from the kibbutz out of the wreck of their transport and then he'd lifted the overturned lorry off his old comrade, who escaped the explosion which followed by only seconds. Ted could try to pooh-pooh the acclaim as much as he wanted, he'd deserved that Israeli medal and he deserved the one he'd get because of his bravery in putting out this fire just as much. She only hoped she and Dorothy could be there when Commander Cushman pinned it on him. It would be wonderful if her fiancé Ron could be too. The four of them together again, just like when they'd been marooned together, back in May.

"Ted you guys put out that fire just in time. It could have

touched off a whole ready locker full of ammunition and rockets, *dangerous* ordnance material!"

Bates picked up the thread of the conversation, "So Sam, you're tellin' me that Judy and I are gettin' medals too?"

"Yes Billy, along with Marty, Stef, Pam and Dorothy. Get used to it my friend, maybe the award will jack up your multiple so it'll be easier for you to make first class. By the way, have you thought about putting in for duty as an instructor?"

Bates was aghast, "Hadn't thought of that Sam."

Wilson had an idea and took the bone in her teeth, "I know the *perfect* billet for you Billy and it's a good thing too, because Judy can go to the same duty station!"

Obenauf perked right up, "Where can we go together Sam?"

"Easy Judy! You can both come to Annapolis, *with me!*"

CHAPTER 7
THE DUPE

ENSIGN MICHAEL NAGLE WAS THE newest officer in the battle group. He had graduated from NROTC in the early summer and had spent the intervening months, before reporting aboard, at Newport, Rhode Island attending basic Surface Warfare Officer's school. There he had scored somewhere near the middle of the pack in all of his academic courses. However he had distinguished himself, among all of his classmates, in one area; and of course this had come to the attention of his instructors. He had achieved the unenviable standing of: "Asshole of the Week" by garnering the most votes in the AOW one-cent-per-vote contest as contributed by all his peers in the training course.

One of the instructors, upon discovering and receiving an invitation to cast his vote in the novel contest, had immediately dropped a sawbuck on Nagle after a particularly inept performance during a session involving a very rudimentary operation with a maneuvering board, thereby sealing the young man's fate for him over the rest of his term in the school.

As the course progressed, he won so often that in the waning weeks, his peers had elevated him to Asshole *Emeritus* status in an attempt to stimulate more competition in the voting, for other deserving candidates. At a penny per vote, Nagle had generated enough cash in the huge glass jar where all the change and bills were collected, to purchase several rounds of drinks for the other twenty five men in his class and their instructors, at the Coaster's Harbor Island Officers club bar.

In all fairness however, Mister Nagle had been born with only a moderate share of the asshole gene, but this was more than compensated for by a colossal chunk of the naïveté one and a vast helping of the clumsiness one. His genetic material loadout had so depleted the available supplies at the gullibility and awkwardness distribution centers that there was nothing left for the next fifty applicants. If one could have peered into the mind of Mr. Phineas T. Barnum, one would have seen the figure of young Michael Nagle, propped up in the front of the meeting room, as Barnum lectured his acolytes in how to separate a sucker from his cash. Nagle was the hayseed of hayseeds, the rube of rubes and everybody knew it. You could dress him in any uniform you wanted and it would only mask his ineptitude for a short time. His stripes revealed themselves instantly whenever he was called upon to perform any act one could reasonably expect of a naval officer. Sizing up the situation, figuring out what to do, giving orders and instruction to his sailors, these were his real weaknesses. Dropping him into the middle of an emergent situation, shipboard or ashore where he had to act, where others might turn to him for leadership? *Disastrous!*

His instructors shuddered to think that this novice might be called upon to actually *lead* any sailors he might be appointed over. The senior seamanship instructor had nightmares when he considered what might happen on a ship where Nagle was picked to oversee even the most rudimentary shipboard evolution. He tried to imagine him supervising the anchor detail and could only picture the "Keystone Cops" in one of their "pre-talkie" adventures as the paddy wagon raced without it's driver, to crash into something and plunge over the side of a bridge, while all the "cops" chased after it with their drawn Billy clubs in their hands.

The senior tactics instructor even dubbed the disastrous seventeen-ship collision that the young man had caused in the ship tactical trainer: a "Nagle," and the epithet immediately became the metric for all things that were fouled up. It was followed in their vernacular by additions of; the "Half Nagle", the "Total Nagle" and the never-to-be-used lightly, the "Fuckin' *Complete* Nagle". The senior navigation instructor even considered naming the basket where he kept the dumbest answers to the weekly celestial navigation practical works: the "Nagletorium". Neither of those officers could recommend sending Nagle to the fleet in any capacity *other than*, as a bad example.

The commanding officer of the school collected all the comments and recommendations from his department heads and found himself in a quandary. On the one hand, the taxpayers had ponied up a considerable chunk of cash to train this turkey and the bureau of personnel would give him fits if his pipeline didn't burp out the appropriate number of JOs—junior officers—to man the ships in the fleet. On the other, he considered busting him out of the class for unsuitability and sending him off to a part of the navy where he couldn't embarrass anyone, but his academic achievements precluded that. He'd even thought of keeping him there at Newport on some pretext or other. On second thought though, he already had an officer in charge of the swimming pool and one in charge of the hardly-ever-used-gear locker. Still, if he put him in charge of one of their deep sinks, the instructional staff would be happy because he could continue to generate cash in the voting, and the rounds of free drinks might continue.

The commanding officer was able to rationalize his reluctance to retain the hapless Nagle by remembering that the role of every chief petty officer in the navy includes the responsibility for essentially "training" every new young officer. He remembered how nervous he'd felt as a "fresh caught" ensign, newly reported to his first at sea billet in a destroyer. His first chief was a grizzled veteran of three wars and it was under his patient, nurturing tutelage that he had overcome any shyness he'd experienced in front of the men in his division.

Chief Mann had shown him the ropes, gradually helping him to understand the functioning of the division's equipment and keeping the sailors from suspecting he was a non-experienced nobody, while making him feel like he was actually running the division. Hey it hadn't been that long until he'd been able to stand a taught watch on the bridge or on the quarterdeck in port. Hell, he'd turned out pretty well! But then again he'd at least known not to take an instruction from a senior that would send him scurrying off to find the ship's storekeepers in search of forty fathoms of waterline. Surely he had known never to volunteer to help his roommate go after the affections of a young woman by collecting a bouquet of compass roses.

He'd figured that out with the encouragement of the senior watch officer, Lieutenant Commander Barnes. Surely there must still be Chief Manns and Mr. Barneses on every ship in the navy! Leaders with the capacity for instructing, the patience and the stamina to help this young officer until he got his sea legs under him and knew his way around the ship and his responsibilities to his ship and the men in his division. Well maybe that was setting his sights a little high, in Nagle's case he'd be satisfied if the young man could learn his way back to his own stateroom … from the head.

In the end, the taxpayers won out and the Bureau of Personnel cut the orders sending Ens. Michael D. Nagle (his contemporaries were convinced that the "D" actually stood for "DIPSTICK") and he departed that Friday, bound for the Mediterranean and the next ship in line to receive a newly minted Ensign. His air transport would arrive in Rota Spain where he would spend the night billeted in the bachelor officer's quarters. He would not have the opportunity to run up much of a bar tab though, by chance he would run into a base administrative officer there and he was able to link him up with his flight to destiny. With that lucky break he would be able to catch *Eisenhower's* COD flight, on it's way to return to the battle group. It landed on *Ike's* flight deck the day before she anchored in Algiers and a helo transferred him, with all his luggage, to his ultimate destination that very afternoon.

USS Porter wasn't expecting it, but when the helo landed on her fantail it deposited nine hundred pounds of cargo (mostly spare parts), a bag of mail, and one ensign. In retrospect, perhaps it might have been better if it had been: spare parts, mail and a bale of rags; but no matter, the young officer instantly became the most junior one aboard and would automatically inherit all of the onerous "SLJO" duties. He would be carried on the ship's books as the Assistant EMO and would command the attention of the senior watch officer for the foreseeable future. He would be tapped immediately to perform every function that was considered to be a bad deal by all the other officers, both shipboard and ashore.

CHAPTER 8
A SPECIAL INVITATION

"SAM CAN YOU SPARE A moment?"

She almost never got a phone call from the captain so she immediately answered, "Yes Sir", put down the phone and headed for his cabin. It wasn't often that her boss interrupted her routine, he must be in a hurry for something she hadn't anticipated. She knocked on his door and he invited her inside.

"Good morning Captain, how was the reception at the Presidential Palace last night?"

He smiled shaking his head, "They had a native group for the entertainment Sam. Girls in veils and pantaloons and men with scimitars, headdresses and pantaloons too. I guess it was supposed to be Ali Baba or something, but the admiral and I were pretty much not into it. You've spoiled us with the show you're putting on and I haven't even seen it yet. Listen I need you to put on a special bit of the show tonight for the ambassador and his party and some of the Algerian officials and their wives. There should be a dozen of them, could you do say a half hour of it, starting at 2000?"

She was almost floored by the request, they hadn't done even one complete walk through of the show and the women's costumes were still in the dying and sewing stage, the set was only half-way built and painted on the hangar deck, and she had no idea who in the cast or their orchestra was available for this evening. But she knew Bates would be aboard and a couple more of the Tars and the 'Midshipmite' and Pam Carbury was a "cousin", maybe she could string together enough to put on the introduction and pull in the master chief as her Sir Joseph understudy. She would need part of the orchestra too. Please God, let Chief Owens and the PMC who was her "Buttercup" be here and it might work.

"I think I can do it Captain, the admiral can't do his part I know, but I've got his understudy and I think I can have enough of the cast and orchestra to squeak out at least some partial numbers. Can I have a few minutes to see who I've got for sure?"

The captain chuckled, "Sam, the admiral *is* available for you, and if you can do it, I'm inviting *Porter* and *Montpelier* too, at least a few of them."

She was as excited as she'd been in the fifth grade when she'd trounced that bitchy little Ruthie Evans in the school spelling bee, nailing every word and winning with the rarely heard: "porcine" which she had thought totally appropriate, in reference to her opponent. "I'll be back in ten minutes Captain."

She raced off and phoned the chief's quarters from her office. She found out Chief Owens was aboard and so was Chief Sutton, her Buttercup. She called the flag spaces and found that the flag sec was aboard and anxious to lead her orchestra that evening, she was having a special practice after lunch and most of the players would be available. Things were really looking up. She called the CDO next and had him announce that there would be a special practice performance by the *Pinafore* cast that night on the hangar deck at 2000 and the players should muster with her at *"Pinafore* headquarters" at 1900. She crossed her fingers and went back to see the captain.

"I can do it Boss. It may be spotty but I've got enough of the people to pull it off. The set is only half-way and I'm short most of the women's costumes but the audience should be able to watch twenty minutes of it easy."

"Sam the miracle worker! By the way those 1650's were perfect thank you."

"I had Marty do most of it Captain, I just made the template for her and told her how important it was. I think she'll be outstanding. Oh I bought my mom a rug yesterday would you like to see it? For the price, I thought I got an outstanding deal."

He came to her office and she unbundled the rug for him to look over. She really did get a bargain in his opinion. She gave him the name and address of the shop and he laughed when she described how she had negotiated with Achmed. It was classic Sam. He only hoped he could do half as well on his own.

The rest of the day was a whirlwind of scurrying about, looking after all the loose ends and getting things in place for the evening's performance. She was surprised to find that she was nowhere near as bad off as she had thought in the costume department. All the men's costumes were finished already and the women's dresses and hats had become top priority with the petty officer in charge of the uniform shop. They had sewn almost all of them but still needed to do the final fittings on her female members. Only Buttercup's and Hebe's costumes were really ready.

Wilson went to the orchestra practice after lunch and found that only one of their guitar players was ashore. If they played anywhere nearly as good as they did in the practice that evening it would be *outstanding,* at least musically. She took a tour on the hangar deck and found that her set was coming along nicely too. The quarterdeck and the faux "gun turret" were finished and the carpenters had primed the plywood and canvas scenery, they only needed the final coat of paint to be ready. Even the mast with it's flag hoist was up and ready. Wilson found the chief and thanked him for the incredible job his people had done.

He laughed, "Sam they were happy to do it, it's not often that we get to do something really creative. The troops would rather work on this than on any of their normal projects. Your show is great fun for them."

The EMC whose team was setting up their stage lighting had most of the lights in place and the temporary cables were strung too. They would be able to light the set and whatever wasn't up to snuff for tonight's show could easily be taken care of, well in advance of their official "opening night".

Wilson knew she would need to build an extensive list of all the show's contributors. No wonder the "credits" that ran after a movie took up so much time.

She found her friend Bev the hairdresser in the barber shop. She was the one who headed her show's "makeup department". She and two other SHs would be available to help get her cast made up and she would set up their "makeup central" in the *Pinafore* headquarters at 1900. The cast members would be treated to their best efforts.

By the time she got around to supper she was too excited to eat. Even a trip back to her office resulted in good news. Marty had taken a phone call from Mr. Parker and his wife who had come out to the ship early, to take advantage of the promised tour. She had met them at the quarterdeck and had enlisted one of the chiefs in the operations department to show them around. She had told them that Sam was busy at that time but she was sure they would be able to see her later during the show.

Even better, there was a new letter from Ron and he was happy to report that his football team had won the two scrimmage games they'd played. He had done well and hadn't been injured. He'd even thrown three touchdown passes and he was happy with that. He was crazy about her, he missed her and hoped she wasn't too bored running everything in the battle group. His tongue-in-cheek statement was so ironic that she had to laugh.

She heard the announcements of *Montpelier* and *Porter* arriving aboard and knew that they would be having dinner in the captain's mess shortly. She thought she'd better go get squared away and into her costume for the show. She had a period British navy lieutenant's costume with its full blue coat, white waistcoat and knee-length breeches. A pair of white pantyhose would make it look authentic. She would be able to pace the "quarterdeck" on the set and appear to be part of the cast, while in reality she would be cuing the tunes and moving the show along.

It only took her a few minutes to don her costume, put her hair back into a "club", and make it to the lounge where the makeup crew, was "making up", *her* crew! She found Bates in front of the mirror table with two of the women who were making up his cheeks. The heavy rouge on his ebony skin made her want to laugh but she realized that the stage lighting would require it. His costume was perfect. He was the quintessential Bill Bobstay right down to his button-front bell bottoms and his bo'sun's pipe with its white cord looped 'round his neck. The flat hat with its HMS PINAFORE ribbon round it was perfect. Gosh her wardrobe department was good! Most of her Tars were in their costumes already. Together they looked fabulous with their square-necked jumpers and their striped undershirts. Chief Owens was donning his captain's costume and she could see that it fit him like a glove. His gold lace and his epaulettes looked like the real thing and his fore and aft hat had a wonderfully fluffy white plume and when he put it on his head he looked very dashing. Most of the women's dresses were done too but the girls had to pin themselves together. This was the perfect way to make those last minute corrections in advance. She thought that the path to their real opening night would be very leisurely, based on what she was seeing tonight. And then Admiral Townsend walked in wearing his beautiful waistcoat and breeches. He would don his great gilded coat when they all went up to the hangar deck.

Sam wasn't sure why he hadn't gone to the formal dinner but this was a windfall for the show. "Admiral how nice to have you aboard Sir!"

He turned when he heard her voice, "Sam you look marvelous." It sounded like MAWWVLUSS because he was already in character.

She giggled and curtsied, "Why thank you m'lord! I see that your waistcoat is finished and may I say Sir, *quite* handsome!"

She signaled for her makeup supervisor, "Bev can you see to Sir Joseph's cheeks and hair my deeaahh?" The excitement of the upcoming show and the camaraderie of the company in their rush to get ready was making them all a little giddy.

Wilson knew it would be fun as she led all of them to the hangar deck in their costumes, her "Tars" toting the swabs that they would dance with in their opening number. Even her friend the admiral's chief of staff stood by the companionway to wish them well as they trouped up the ladder to entertain the embassy staff and the captains of the ships nested in the roadstead with them.

There were calls of "Kick ass Sam!" "C'mon Admiral, we're all rootin' for ya!", "Yeah Chief Owens!" and "Go for it Bad Billy!" Everyone had forgotten that the non-jinxing way to wish them well was: "Break a leg!"

With the stage lighting on and their audience seated in the temporary seating that the master chief had rushed to the hangar deck, the orchestra took it's place by the set. From the opening strains of the overture, through the final notes of "*…for he is an Englishman, he remains an Englishman!*" their audience was enthralled by the spirited production. The tar's dance while maneuvering their swabs in choreographed unison was excellent and showed how hard Chief Owens had worked to make that part of the production both authentic and entertaining.

The arrival of Sir Joseph with his entourage of women relatives was riotously funny. Bill Bobstay gave the most authentic and hilarious pipe anyone had ever heard. He began as the august peer put his toe onto the quarterdeck and held the trill while each of the sisters, cousins and aunts swept aboard in their colorful finery. Bates had run out of breath when there were still three "aunts" to go. His comic drawing of a huge breath to continue had the audience in stitches and the follow-on Sir Joseph's *"I am the Monarch of the seas…"* and his rollickingly funny *"When I was a lad I served a term as office boy in an attorney's firm…"* had the audience holding their sides.

Wilson hardly had to cue anyone at all. Only her Josephine, one of the lieutenants from the supply department, needed any real reminding of her lines. Wilson was proud of them all. The individual songs and arias were as good as any light opera company had ever produced, she was sure of that, and her chorus of sisters, cousins, aunts, sailors and marines was exceptional. She could see that the men from *Montpelier* who had joined the embassy visitors and a few *Porter* sailors really loved the show. Ted and the other men who had helped during the night of the fire were the captain's special guests and of course Dorothy was there too, bubbling over with excitement for her friend.

They ran through the entire production, much more than the captain had asked for, and the applause afterward made it all worthwhile. The cast gathered round Wilson and the admiral. She had coaxed him into playing the comic lead in the show and she knew that because he had been so good-natured and had embraced the show, everyone from all the ships in the battle group would want to come and attend when they put the show on during their turnover period at Rota. Obviously they couldn't crowd everyone in by the stage on the hangar deck. Even with all the planes and equipment moved out of the way to make as much space as possible, they would only be able to have a couple of thousands of their friends in attendance. The solution seemed to her to have more than one performance. The problem with that of course was that it cut into the time that the admiral and the other important cast members would have to spend away from their "real" normal duties. She would have to figure out how to arrange the multiple shows. Maybe they could do it the navy way, of course! "Admiral you were so good we'll have to have two shows during turnover to crowd everyone in. We'll have to have a "Gold show" and a "Blue show" that's the only way we'll be able to fit everybody in."

"Sir Joseph" was in an expansive mood following his triumphant performance and answered her quickly, "Sam I'm quite sure you're right and I'd hate to slight our reliefs. I'm sure you'll figure a way to pull off both performances."

Many of *Ike's* crew had crowded in behind the audience to steal a sneak-preview of the show, so the after show cast party was a raucous event. Wilson was handed a beverage in a paper cup by the command master chief. It sure tasted a lot like the wine she'd tasted in Greece. Apparently the master chief's abilities to arrange support for the cast and crew in the show knew no bounds and she drank hers surrounded by an appreciative cast.

It was after that that the Ambassador's wife invited the admiral, the captains, and a few officers from each of the ships, back to the embassy the following evening and she reminded Commander Cushman of his promise to provide the long-awaited and highly anticipated, *Gandhi*.

CHAPTER 9
HOT REELIN'

WILSON HAD COLLECTED HER FRIENDS at her office after they had finished work for the day and Manckowicz had arrived to escort them aboard. They were all invited for dinner aboard *Montpelier* and she knew that the menu for the evening included one of her favorites, "J5s", the submariner's cut of beef that they loved best because it was done precisely to a turn and served like a ribeye steak, no "mystery meat" there; piping hot on the white crockery plates that the sub sailors got to use. They didn't have the big stainless steel trays they had on *Ike* and *Porter*, because the sub didn't have the giant automatic dishwashers that surface ships used. Theirs was a dinky little thing that could only hold standard sized dinner plates.

Wilson liked the small, intimate feel of the sub's crew's mess too. There were only eight tables, not the hundred or so that *Ike* had. It was kinda neat, everybody knew everybody else on the sub. On *Ike* there were hundreds of people at chow every day and they had no idea who most of the others were. She tried to explain it to the other women, "It's just so much cozier having supper on *Monty*. There's no pressure to hurry and eat so others can take your seat for their turn. Also when the sub's guys talk to you they're nice, it's not like they're trying to hit on you all the time, like some of the sailors on *Ike* seem to be."

Stanfield laughed as she nodded in agreement, "Sam's right girls, I spent a whole week with them at Ashdod and they were all very nice to me." She giggled then, "Of course if they hadn't been, Teddy would have had something to say about it." She reached her hand up to the big blonde sailor's forehead and rumpled his hair, bringing on his sheepish grin.

Fernandez and Carbury watched Stanfield's caressing of her fiancé and marveled at the ability of the beautiful diminutive woman sailor to so completely mesmerize the broad-shouldered, good-natured submariner, that boy was *definitely hers!*

As they began their walk toward the submarine moored alongside Wilson asked Turner how she was coming along on her paperwork for the commissioning program, "So Steph how are you doing on the paper to get to be an officer?"

"I'll finish when we leave Algiers Sam, I already interviewed with Captain Sweeney and he seemed quite positive."

Stanfield heard her and volunteered a thought to Turner, "Whatever you do Steph, don't go to the school our new ensign went to, some of the men in our radar division were saying he's a catastrophe waiting to happen."

The ensuing laughter garnered stories about other officers they had known who had not covered themselves with glory in some pretty funny situations. During supper, one of the *Monty* men told the story of a young ensign who had tried to report aboard when they were at the pier in New London, only to discover the next morning that he'd checked aboard the wrong boat. The chief yeoman had discovered it the next day when he'd opened the officer's package and found the original of his orders inside, sending him to the boat just across the pier.

All of the *Monty* sailors were friendly and of course they were starved for women's company. Even though they had gotten a chance to meet Stanfield and Wilson, because they'd spent a couple of days underway together, the novelty of having women sailors aboard had not worn off. So the crew had eagerly accepted them and it was a huge bonus that there were more of *Ike's* women sailors that Wilson had introduced them too. The way they had all pitched in to help the other night had sure made the difference in fighting that fire! They would all be great shipmates, if only women could serve on submarines.

They were sitting together just after supper and clean up in *Montpelier's* crew's mess. The original six "fire eating females," the women sailors who had helped with the fire on *Ike's* weather deck two nights ago. They'd had an excellent supper with their *Monty* friends and Stanfield was holding hands with her fiancé as they made loving eyes at each other at an outboard table.

The duty chief had just made his tour of the boat and pronounced it clean enough and he gave RM2 Warner the 'okay' sign. "Go ahead Warner, roll the flick."

"I'm on it Chief. Somebody get the lights!"

And with those few words the epic's panoramic opening scene flickered onto the pull-down screen at the forward end of the crew's mess. But it was only a few moments after that that the duty officer arrived, short of breath, to make his fateful announcement. "Hold it up Chief, we've got a problem, the XO told me that he'd promised *Porter's* XO they could watch *Gandhi* in their wardroom tonight."

There was an audible groan from the men and women in the mess. The lights flicked back on and Warner stopped the projector. This was an unexpected glitch and it caught all of them in the crew's mess unawares. It was then that Wilson remembered what Commander Cushman had said to the ambassador's wife as they were congratulating her cast on the hangar deck, after the show the evening before.

She got the young lieutenant's attention with a hand wave, "Sir, last night Commander Cushman promised the ambassador's wife that the embassy could watch *Gandhi* tonight after their banquet. It sure seems like the movie is oversubscribed for tonight."

Manckowicz had heard the captain's commitment too, "Mr. Leech, Sam's right, I was standing right by the captain when he promised it to them and the ambassador's wife was really happy when he did. She even hugged him when he said it."

MM2 Crandall was sitting right next to Warner and he made the pragmatic suggestion emblematic of his nuclear-trained, problem-solving mind. "Hey Mr. Leech it's easy, we'll just 'hot reel' the flick. We'll rewind the first reel while Warner threads the next one in the projector and someone can hand carry it over to *Porter*. They can watch it, rewind it, and send it ashore. Somebody can take it from the landing to the embassy by taxi and they can watch it too!"

The utter genius of Crandall's proposition, at least in the young lieutenant's mind, leapt the gap between "hair-brained scheme" and "stupendous suggestion" and was all that was needed to convince him to execute the idea. It would enable all three groups of movie-aficionados to see the film, it would get his XO off the hook with *Porter*, and his CO would be GOLDEN in the eyes of the embassy ladies. Sure it would take a couple of extra steps and there would be a few minute delay between each reel as the successive one was re-wound and transported to the next viewing sight, but it *would work!*

Leech would make sure he gave Crandall credit for the idea. The biggest hassle would be *Porter's* anyway, they would have to find someone who could get the reels from the ship to the landing safely, then they'd have to rely on the Algerian cab drivers. Hey, *Porter* had her own boats, it should be a piece of cake. After all, "hot reeling" was a regularly accepted way of doing business. They'd just done it with *Grease* the other night, between the crew's mess and the wardroom.

The lieutenant nodded and made his pronouncement, "Okay, who's going to run the reels over to *Porter?*"

Manckowicz looked over at TM3 Lupo, "Lupo make yourself useful for once in your life. Think you can find your way up the brow, across *Ike's* hangar deck and down the starboard accommodation ladder to *Porter?*"

Lupo recognized his vulnerability in this situation. If he acquiesced and agreed to do it, he would have to hump each reel of the movie up three decks, across the hangar deck and down two decks to *Porter*, he'd miss the first five minutes of each successive reel. On the other hand if he *didn't* agree, Manckowicz would probably tie his arms and legs in a knot and drop-kick his ass off the sail to the other side of the bay. The choice was easy. "Sure thing Mank. Hey Mr. Leech you can count on me, I'll get the reels over to *Porter*, no problem."

"Alright then, roll the flick Warner."

Thirty five minutes later the last frame of reel one was pulled past the aperture of the sturdy Bell and Howell's lens and the familiar slap, slap, slap; as the bitter end of the celluloid contacted the winder arm, caused Warner to stop the projector and remove the now-empty reel from the rear sprocket. He passed it to Lupo who put it on the rewinder.

Every ship had a rewinder, it consisted of a board with two sprocket arms attached, a rewind sprocket and a "dead man". The rewinder had a crank and handle on it which drove the sprocket through a set of tiny gears. The operator of the rewinder just had to use plenty of elbow grease to spin the empty reel, thereby pulling the film off the dead man onto the rewind reel, resulting in a fully rewound reel, ready to be projected or placed in its hard olive-green movie storage container which would then be fastened closed with a pair of webbed straps with metal buckles.

Lupo took the full-and-now-backwards reel, placed it on the dead man sprocket and began hand-cranking the machine. The growing volume of film on the rewind reel was matched by the shrinking volume on the dead man. In a matter of moments the reel was restored to it's fully ready condition, just as Wilson and Fernandez returned from their visit to the head in the chief's quarters.

Warner fired up the second reel as Lupo headed up the ladder on his way to *Porter*. There he turned the reel over to their quarterdeck watch and told him he'd bring the next one in a half hour or so. Everything seemed to be going just fine.

The bulk of her officers were assembled in *Porter's* wardroom to watch the much-anticipated film. Only the captain, the XO and one other officer were absent; but they would see the film at the embassy. The senior watch officer remarked that the three were probably also being treated to some form of adult beverage during the showing. Others who had hoped to attend with *Porter's* contingent groused that there were probably women there too.

One of the mess attendants rolled the first reel moments after he returned from the quarterdeck with it. The aroma of popcorn and a mood of expectant enthusiasm prevailed as the relaxing officers settled in for the evening's entertainment.

Another of the mess attendants had been tapped to take the rewound reels and give them to the cox'n of the captain's waiting gig who would convey them to the landing. There his bowhook would jump into the next available taxi and deliver them to the eagerly expectant party at the embassy. The senior watch officer remarked to his friends in the wardroom that their quickly arranged handoff method reminded him of the legendary "Tinker to Evers to Chance", the double play maestros of the Chicago Cubs, who had confounded all other teams in the National League during the years when they'd been a power house. He was right of course, but he'd forgotten what happened … after Tinker, et al went home for the night.

Aboard *Montpelier* the night's entertainment went off without a hitch. The projector had just been cleaned and lubricated, it's bulb was brand spanking new, the pulleys were sure and true and held the segmented spring-drive chain taut; the machine performed it's function flawlessly. The ship had another projector too and they would have pressed it into service, had there been a problem, but it was older, noisier and not as reliable as the one they'd used this evening; so it was relegated to use by the wardroom and was stored there under the watchful eye of the IC division officer.

After Warner ran the last reel and handed it to Lupo to hump over to *Porter*, he set the two halves of the hard olive-green movie storage case aside while he re-stowed the crew's projector in it's normal locker. He would keep the case there on the outboard rear table bench seat in the crew's mess until they brought the reels back later. Then someone could put them in the case and re-stow it in it's normal rack, with all the other films.

CHAPTER 10
WAJID'S TAXI

THE AMBASSADOR AND HIS WIFE stood in the foyer to wish all of their guests a good night. The admiral departed first along with his chief of staff and the flag operations officer. They thanked their hostess for the superb dinner and the wine. Since the entertainment had really been provided by *Montpelier* it didn't seem right to thank her for that but it had been her idea and it had been an enjoyable time watching the film with them all, so the admiral graciously said he'd enjoyed it. The *Eisenhower* officers walked out next and Captain Christensen, his air officer and his Protestant chaplain were effusive in their thanks. *Montpelier's* officers followed and they remarked at length about the superb cuisine. When they were at sea submerged, fresh produce was a rarity and the great salads they'd had during their banquet made them all think of home.

Porter's officers departed last and the ladies of the embassy staff were fussing over the newest and most junior member who had seemed polite and very accommodating during supper. They had seated him next to the junior assistant attaché for agricultural affairs because they had learned that he was a graduate of an obscure Midwestern university, who had majored in something that no one had ever heard of. As he approached the ambassador's wife to give her his thanks, the XO turned and reminded him of the real reason he had been included in *Porter's* contingent.

"Mr. Nagle make sure you get those reels and get them back to

Montpelier tonight. Those sub sailors sure did a fine job of making their movie available and our troops jumped through hoops to get it here so we could see it. It's the least we can do to get it back to them tonight and in great shape. Make sure you get *the whole* movie too. It'll probably take the embassy man a while to rewind the reels but it's considered the polite thing to do, rewinding the film before putting it away. It's like washing the Tupperware before returning it to your neighbor down the street when she brings over her prized recipe for the neighborhood picnic. I'll send the captain's gig back to get you, it'll be waiting at the landing for you by the time you get there."

Nagle said his aye, ayes and indicated that he knew what to do. He retreated to the large room where they had watched the epic and found that the embassy's projectionist was almost finished rewinding the first of the reels. He seemed to know what he was about and the young officer let him proceed without interruption. The stack of rewound film reels continued to grow as he watched but then he was overwhelmed by the need to relieve himself. The embassy's man directed him to the appropriate facility where he availed himself quickly of it and returned to find that the rewinding was complete. The projectionist then indicated that he had received the reels individually and he hadn't received a container for them. But he would attempt to find a suitable vessel to hold them all on his journey back to the ship.

The callow ensign understood and waited while the helpful embassy staffer went off in search of something that would hold the fourteen-inch reels of film. By then all the offices on the lower floor of the building were shut and locked and the suitable pickings were lean. At last he found an unlocked door and a filing cabinet full of shipping and mailing materials. He made his selection and returned to the projection area to find the waiting courier. The chosen container was a cardboard box, sufficient in size to handle the reels, and it was a lucky find; nothing else substantial was available at that hour.

Nagle watched detachedly as the reels were deposited in the box and then the helpful embassy man folded the top shut using the "cross-over-the-flaps method" that most people who have ever moved into or out of a college dorm have used to close a box when there is no adhesive tape or twine to fasten it properly. That method is of course sufficient if one is boxing and transporting sweaters, socks or a few framed photographs of one's loved ones; it is not however recommended for one intent on transporting a dozen pounds of celluloid-filled steel reels.

Nagle thanked the projectionist and took the box from him, supporting it with both hands as he traced the path of his senior officers, out through the vestibule to the entryway. There he encountered his first problem. It is the custom in the navy to remove one's hat when one enters a building and to replace it when leaving. The instructors at OCS had been quite specific about that, but they had not provided any guidance relative to this situation.

Nagle's hat was lying on an ornate table near the door where he had placed it with the others when he'd arrived. It was now the lone occupant of the table and he was unsure how to retrieve it while still maintaining control of the cumbersome carton. How was he supposed to pick up his hat zero-handed? The skirmish between warring ideas that ensued in his mind was finally resolved in favor of custom; he would remain uncovered. Carefully placing the box on the table he lifted his hat and placed it atop the box. Then he lifted the box and hugged it tightly against the gold buttons of his dress whites, his hat balanced precariously, it's brim pressing lightly against his chest.

He shoved the door open with his hip, smiled self-consciously at the marine lance corporal sentry standing at attention just outside the front door, and descended the steps to the street level. A few more paces found him outside the embassy gate on the quiet street, where he was lucky enough to be able to hail the last taxi of the night.

The waiting driver flicked on his headlights when he saw the lone officer exiting the gate, started the wheezing engine of his battered Citroen, and pulled forward 'til he was even with the uniformed man. These American sailors had proven to be very good for his business over the past several days. He only hoped that their ships would remain in the harbor for a long time. His uncles, brothers and cousins were all reaping the benefits too and his share of the commission on the exorbitant souvenir trinkets in the waterfront shops was an added bonus.

He was counting on that income to finance his early retirement and he was sure that the wives he would amass by then would choose the perfect site for him to build his dreamed of palace, when he finally hung up his car keys and switched to dealing in camels, as his ancestors had. This lone American officer looked like an easy mark for an egregious fare, if there was any resistance he would remind him that it was late and transporting the box was an extra.

Nagle angled gingerly toward the rear door and somehow managed to steady the box as he prized up on the handle with an unoccupied finger. He managed to open it a crack and jockeyed his body and the box around the edge of the partially opened door. He jammed the tip of his right elbow into the space between the door and the door post, congratulating himself on his newfound dexterity. Then, with a confident backward thrust of his elbow, he flung wide the door and was in sight of his goal. All he had to do was place the box on the rear seat and slide it across as he glided in beside it.

It was at that very instant that his genetic curse chose to strike. Perhaps it was the overconfidence, but more likely it was his affliction, rising to the surface once more.

Nagle stumbled and lurched forward causing his hat to slide off the box, bounce against the door post and land on the sidewalk beside the taxi. In a panic to retrieve his errant cover he tossed the box onto the back seat where it bounced and toppled forward, landing on the floor and bursting open. The reels landed on the floor in disarray and one of them slid under the front seat.

The embarrassed young officer recovered his hat and brushed off the white cover. It appeared no worse for wear and he put it on his head, pulling it tightly down so it wouldn't fall off. He leaned in and retrieved the box, placing it on the seat and then reached down, retrieving the errant reels, placing them in the box one at a time … all three of them. The driver looked at him through his rear view mirror, "Monsieur ees quite reddeee now, oui?"

Nagle slid in and shut the door, "Yes I'm ready to go now."

"To thee sheeps no?"

"Yes take me to the landing please."

The engine wheezed faster as the taxi pulled away from the curb. The driver accelerated down the street and followed a well-known but circuitous route back to the landing. It took a few minutes longer than a simple straight-line route but the driver was sure he had confused the vacuous officer sitting in the rear. He had already decided on the fare he would attempt to extort. When he pulled up next to the little shore patrol shack it's lights were on and he could see there were some Americans inside. He would have to fleece this passenger quickly and quietly so as not to draw them into the negotiation.

Nagle could see that the land portion of his mission was completed and opened the rear door reaching for the box with the reels inside. He got out of the cab taking the box with him and placed it on the ground by his feet as he reached for his wallet.

"How much do I owe you Sir?"

"Eeet ees trois mille dinars Monsieur; how you say, tree towwsannd dinars."

Nagle hadn't a clue what the exchange rate was from dollars and he had none of the elaborate dinar notes with their pictures of dead, mustachioed Algerian heroes so he pulled a twenty out of his wallet. "Will this cover it?"

"Non Monsieur, another of those weel be enuff."

The second twenty changed hands quickly and the driver drove off, happy with his evening's work. He would get a good night's sleep and meet his brothers, cousins and uncles for coffee tomorrow as usual.

Nagle picked up the box and made his way to the landing stairs,

Porter's gig was sitting alongside ready to take him back to the anchorage. He used care descending to the level of the floating dock and the bowhook helped him over the gun'l and into the sternsheets. His trip out to the flagship was uneventful and he disembarked at the boom. The bowhook gave him a hand again and the boat crew saw him ascending the boarding ladder with the cardboard box held tightly under his left arm. He used his right to grab the hand rail, the last thing he needed at this point was to slip and drop the box into the harbor. Based on the look the XO had given him, he was sure if *anything* went over the side it had better be him.

He was able to salute the national ensign and the OOD and even offered the box up for inspection, but the watch waved him on. He made his way across the hangar deck to the ladder that ran down to the deck of the submarine. It was a quick trip down the ladder where he was met on deck by a petty officer wearing dungarees and armed with a holstered pistol. Nagle remembered to salute the ensign and then the watch in just the nick of time.

He greeted the sub's topside watch, "Good evening, I'm Ensign Nagle from the *Porter*, I've brought your movie back from the embassy. Can you take it or should I wait for the movie officer?"

TM3 Lupo had never heard of a "movie officer" so he answered quickly, "I got it Sir, no problem."

The box changed hands immediately. Lupo took it, placed it on the deck under the communications suitcase, and logged the ensign's name and the time of the event in the topside log.

The hapless officer made his way back to *Porter* where he found the XO in the wardroom, just spooning the last of his ice cream into his mouth. "Sir I just took the movie over to the sub and turned it over to them. Everything's fine XO, it sure was a great film!"

Aboard *Montpelier* it was time for watch change and Lupo was anxious for MM3 Burton to hurry his ass up so he could get relieved and grab some mid-rats. They had two more days here and he wanted to take advantage of the time ashore too. When Burton finally made his way topside Lupo gave him his standard relief spiel, "I had it, you got it and here's your gun."

He drew the Colt from it's holster and pulled back the slide, demonstrating that the pistol was safe and empty. Burton nodded and Lupo re-holstered the piece, unhooked the hooks on the guard belt and passed it to Burton. He fumbled a few moments letting out the belt two hook's worth to accommodate his larger girth, and fastened it about his own waist. Lupo kept up a patter as he scribbled his relieving entry in the topside watch log book, "Kinda hard to see the draft marks aft with the overhang of *Ike's* deck blockin' out the moon and starlight but I s'pose nothin's changed in the past few hours. The harbor is pretty quiet, just the liberty launches runnin back and forth on schedule. The duty officer made his tour a half hour ago and the duty chief will be up in a couple hours. There any sandwich makin's out in the mess?"

"Yeah, pretty good spread actually, excellent soup too. Hey will you ask the night mess cook if he'd mind passin' me up a black and sweet in a half hour or so?"

Lupo was feeling quite expansive now that he'd been relieved, "No problem Burton. Here let me grab this box and run it down to the mess, some drifty ensign from *Porter* brought back our movie. I logged it half an hour ago. Have a good watch, see you in the morning."

Burton watched as the skinny torpedoman stuck his legs down the hatch and paused there while he got the box under one arm before disappearing down the trunk into the operations compartment. He thought, "Crazy damn torpedoman better not screw up that flick or there'll be hell to pay!"

Lupo made it to the crew's mess a few moments later and set the box down on the outboard table near the bench seat where Warner had left the two halves of the empty movie storage case. He made himself a sandwich and ladled out a cupful of the hearty ham-and-split-pea soup that Burton had recommended, then he sat down and dug in. His watch had been a reasonably leisurely one and he reflected back on it. He'd gotten to watch those women sailors head back off to their ships and he'd welcomed the captain, XO and engineer back aboard after their thing at the embassy. Man that damn Manckowicz sure was a lucky sonofabitch, his fiancée was the hottest lookin' woman he'd ever seen and that blonde girl from the carrier was a knockout too. What he wouldn't give for an afternoon with either of them! Too bad he never seemed to be in the right place at the right time.

He finished his snacking and took his cup and dish to the scullery. He was headed off toward his bunk when he remembered Burton's request for a coffee and stuck his head into the galley, "Hey mess crank how 'bout takin' the topside watch a cup o' joe at 0130, a black and sweet?"

The hard working mess cook took his hands out of the ball of dough he was kneading and came to the door, "Okay Lupo I'll do it, on one condition though, you have to get rid of that cardboard box, the chief'll go ape shit if he sees cardboard in here."

Lupo wasn't wild about it, but hey it couldn't hurt and it was pretty simple, "Alright I'll do it, it's as good as gone, just make sure the IC-men re-stow the movie."

"Sure Lupe thanks."

Lupo walked to the table, flipped open the flaps and placed the three reels inside into the bottom half of the case. He found the little movie booklet with it's laminated cover, inside the top half of the case and glanced at it's front: *GANDHI*. Yes he was sure it was the right container and he slid the top half of the case down over the bottom half, inserted the tips of the web belts into their buckles and cinched them tight. He took the cardboard box, slit open the bottom and smashed it flat. Then he took it to the torpedo room and stuffed it into the trash can. It would be tossed out with the other waste during morning clean up ship.

The movie case was sitting on the deck by the crew's mess door when IC2 Corday came in for breakfast at 0515. He had to relieve the below decks watch by 0600 so he didn't have a lot of time to dawdle. He put in his order with the mess cook, "A couple of eggs over easy, some bacon and some home fries please."

The mess cook grabbed a plate and went into the galley to get the requested meal as Corday put two slices of the freshly baked bread into one of the toasters on the rear mess table. Hey it would take a minute or so to brown his toast, maybe he had time to run the movie case back to the rack and put it away. But first he'd make sure, "Hey mess cook, this movie, where'd it come from?"

The young mess cook stuck his head around the galley door and glanced at the case that Corday was now holding by it's carry strap. "That's the flick they showed last night and hot reeled over to the *Porter*. Lupo brought it down last night in a cardboard box and I told him to get rid of the cardboard. He put the reels in that case and cleared out with the box. I put it there when I was getting ready to serve breakfast. It was sitting back there by the projector locker." He pointed toward the well-known location.

"Thanks Rogers, I'll take it from here."

Corday stored the case in the rack with the other movies they'd loaded aboard when they'd left New London and got back to the mess just as his toast popped up. So far it was shaping up to be a pretty decent morning.

CHAPTER 11
AN EARLY DEPARTURE

WILSON AND FERNANDEZ WERE SITTING in the captain's mess with the XO, ready for the morning department head meeting. The XO was telling them that the banquet at the embassy was a good time for all and that the movie afterward had been well received by the embassy staff. It was surely a nice effort on the part of *Montpelier* to accommodate them.

Wilson giggled, "That's pretty amazing XO, Marty and I were on *Monty* last night for dinner and we got to watch the same movie you had at the embassy. They watched it aboard *Porter* too I think."

Fernandez laughed then too, "Sir I'll bet we had as much fun as you did at the embassy."

The XO was interested, "What was on the menu last night, there on *Montpelier* Seaman?"

Her smile was almost a crafty one, "We had steak, potatoes and vegetables Sir; but for dessert I got *three* marriage proposals!"

Wilson was laughing just as hard as the XO was when the last of the department heads arrived and the meeting got underway. It would be a light morning and they would finish their work by the time they had to catch the liberty launch and join those French sailors who had invited them to their ship for Friday's lunch. It would be almost their last day ashore too, since the ship was scheduled to get under way on Monday morning.

She and Fernandez were anxious to see one of the Moorish palaces that were listed in the guidebook. The one that seemed most interesting was way out past the Kasbah on the hillside overlooking the city. Wilson's translation of the French brochure was pretty revealing, the palace had served the Bashaw who was rumored to have had as many as sixty wives. The courtyard there contained some of the most beautiful artwork in all of the Berber world.

They had printed off the "Sam sheets", the detailed notes of the meeting, and made copies for all the departments when the command master chief opened the office door and smiled at Wilson. "Dynamite job you're doing with the show Sam, you know I've heard people in almost every department and division humming the tunes. I told the captain we couldn't have picked a better show or a better sailor to put it on."

Wilson basked and smiled, "Gosh Master Chief when you first tapped me for the job I wasn't sure if I could pull it off. There was so much to learn and so many things to try and get my arms around, but when I read the libretto and saw what the whole story was about I knew it would be fun. And then when I got the admiral to be Sir Joseph, it was the best day I've had in the navy! But, you know that it's been not just a learning experience, it's been a fun experience too."

Connolly gave her a grin, "So what was the learning experience part of it for you Sam?"

She had that right on the tip of her tongue, "Easy, I learned that a good command master chief is a lot like a good captain, he knows everything that's going on and he knows who can do the work and how to inspire them to do it well. And he doesn't get bogged down in the details, he tells the troops what he wants, he treats each of them as an individual, and lets them figure out how to get it done. I guess the best way to say it is he knows how to build and run a team."

The smile that came upon him after she finished was an honest and sincere one and he meant what he was about to say. "Sam the captain is dead-on right about you, you're gonna be an outstanding officer. I'd consider it an honor to serve under you and I may just delay my retirement so I can do just that!"

Wilson was glowing inside at that remark, "Master Chief you are very kind to say that and someday I hope to justify your faith in me. I have to tell you though that when we give the show to the whole crew and the people from *Independence* I intend to give any credit I get to you and I'm having a special costume made up so you can come on stage as one of the cast when they make their final curtain call."

Connolly chuckled, "Just don't make me wear a diaper or anything Sam, and I'll make you a deal, we'll take that bow together, hand in hand." He turned to Fernandez then, "Marty are you going to be able to take over in here when Sam leaves in November?"

She knew what he wanted to hear but she decided to tell him what she really felt, "Master Chief I know I can do the admin mechanical stuff and watching Sam work with all the department heads and the admiral and his staff has taught me a lot about how to get along with people and to help to set the right tone, but really no one can do what Sam does. I'll do everything I can to make the captain's job as easy as I can, but I'll have to be me. I've been working hard on my smile though, and my confidence, and I've been told I'm gaining on it. What do you think?"

He grinned, "I understand you got three marriage proposals the other night. I think that's plenty of progress. All sub sailors?"

She giggled, "Yes Chief, but none of them stood a chance. I told them all I'm married to my job!"

Connolly laughed and patted her on the shoulder, "You're a good sailor Marty. Keep up the excellent work."

He turned back to Wilson, "I hear you're having lunch aboard that French destroyer today."

"We both are Chief, I think the sailors we met were really taken with Marty's exotic eyes and flashing smile. I'm just going along as a chaperone!" She held up her left hand and rotated it displaying her sparkling engagement ring. "I have to go along in case it's really her legs and not her eyes that impressed them."

The master chief laughed his way out of the office and down the passageway. He wished all their sailors were as good as either of those women.

Wilson and her protégée changed into their dress whites and set out for the quarterdeck at 1130. It was a five minute ride to the landing and it was just a few hundred yards up the pier to the *Duquesne's* brow. They climbed it and saluted the petty officer on the quarterdeck whose main function appeared to be security, judging by the machine pistol slung over his shoulder. His hurried phone call soon produced a young man wearing lieutenant's tabs on his collar who spoke excellent English. He escorted the women to the mess decks where they were instantly welcomed. Wilson had never met anyone named Jean Luc before but by the end of the toasts she had met quite a few of them. She met five 'Phillipes' during the main course and added a flock of 'Adrianes' by the end of dessert. Not one of them could hold a candle to her handsome midshipman though, her handsome Ron.

They toured the French ship with their hosts for over an hour and Wilson saw immediately what the captain had hinted at when she had first mentioned going aboard. The whole ship smelled bad and there was dirt and grime almost everywhere she looked. She knew that Master Chief Connolly would have a conniption fit if he saw how under-cleaned the corners of the decks were. She even felt uncomfortable as she climbed ladders with their hosts where balls of dirt seemed to have collected. She wondered if the ship's equipment was in poor condition too. But she realized that this ship represented a big part of France's navy budget and her sailors seemed to be quite proud of her. She did the polite thing and didn't comment on her observations.

They departed amiably and not without souvenirs, Fernandez carried the French sailor's cap she'd been given in exchange for the whitehat she'd brought along just in case she was offered a trade. She still wore her Havelock though, they cost five times as much as a man's whitehat.

Fernandez started first after they were out of earshot, "Sam that ship was *gross!*"

"I know I was just thinking they must not spend much time field daying and some of those guys had *horrible* BO! You know I wonder what they think of our ships, and *us* for that matter!

THE FLIGHT WAS A ROUTINE one, the big P3C Orion aircraft had left the base at Keflavik Iceland that morning right at 0830 and had relieved it's on-station squadron mate in monitoring a LOFAR buoy array in the Norwegian Sea, two hundred miles north of the Hebrides. COMICEASWGRU had been alerted to watch for a transiting Soviet submarine headed south out of the Barents for over a week now and was taking no chances. He had supplemented the routine patrolling by adding the sonobuoy barrier and had put his ace VP Squadron on the job. He was confident that the men of VP 64, his "Condors," could sniff out the new Russian if anybody could. They had a deservedly good reputation and he was happy with their performance as well as their watchful minding of their fuel. They were almost miserly in that expenditure and they didn't toss out expensive sonobuoys like popcorn kernels either.

The much-anticipated Russian sub was their absolute newest and sneakiest and the whole intelligence community was anxious to pounce on one and milk all the data they could from it. They had only gotten tiny tidbits of information about the new class and the great brains in the spook shack were thirsty for more, anything that the sound wizards could glean from an at-sea encounter would be *golden.* He had given everyone notice that he'd spring for drinks at the Keflavik O-club for the crew that first turned up the commie.

AW2 Terry Barrington was highly thought of in the squadron and his popularity transcended the business of flying and finding submerged ships. He was a fantastic pianist and routinely entertained them when he sat down to play in the back room of the enlisted men's club. He had a style that emulated Scott Joplin and he never failed to set their toes to tapping. He had studied music since he was a baby and he'd dreamed of attending Julliard but there hadn't been enough money so he'd enlisted in the navy and had been drawn to his current rating because of the similarity between music and underwater acoustics. He could play the buttons on the acoustical display panel of the AN/AYA-8B system like they were the keys on the big Baldwin piano in the parlor of his folks' house back in Tonawanda. He could watch the recorder monitoring the output of his sixteen sonobuoy array and pick out the slightest anomaly, the faintest hint of a sub.

He had just asked AW1 Barker to spell him for a minute while he went to the head, and was getting his legs under himself to get up from his seat when he saw it, the first indistinct flicker of something not natural, not normal, and not oceanic. It was definitely mechanical, something coming from a machine, a very precise one too. That meant it had to be expensive, probably something that had cost the Politbureau an immense chunk of the motherland's gross national product, something that had cost a ton of rubles. But, even so, it was imparting some tell-tale sound into the water where it spread in all directions, reflecting off the surface and the deep sound channel, losing energy as it's wave front expanded. Nevertheless the physics of the situation were such that the sound pressure level of the noise source was great enough to carry for hundreds of miles and if someone knew what to look for, someone could find it. Terry Barrington knew just exactly what to look for, and his bladder could wait, at least for now.

Barrington made his report to the TACCO who nodded and informed the mission commander. Moments later the watch officer in the ASW Group Operational Control Center had the happy news too and his outgoing message report created a stir in the whole intelligence community. Every intelligence analyst whose desk wasn't already heaped with Secret and Top Secret paper began collecting the information that the VP men had turned up. The Fleet Intel Center included the sub's location in their FICLANT 230500Z OCT 83 LANTINTSUM. Now all the ships who copied the broadcast knew that a Type IV Soviet nuke was at sea and seemed to be headed toward the Atlantic.

For now the Condors would be able to track the slippery sub, but as soon as he crossed through the GIUK Gap and broke out into the Atlantic he would be harder to follow. So far only one noise source could be exploited and none of the traditional ones they were familiar with from older classes of commie nukes seemed to be present in this Bozo. The Commander of PATWINGS FIVE would have to determine which way he was headed, either south, down the Atlantic past the European mainland bound for the Mediterranean, or west toward the coast of the US. He would have to send either his "Seahawks" of VP 23 flying out of Lajes in the Azores, or his "Dragons" from VP 56 staging from Brunswick, Maine. In either case it was a very costly way of gathering data. Every sonobuoy array that was laid only lasted for a brief period because the action of the waves tended to scatter them in every direction and even if it was dead-calm, the batteries only lasted just so long. Each one cost them thousands of dollars and there was all that fuel too, each of those P3Cs had a voracious thirst for the costly liquid even though the pilot feathered one of the four big Allison turbo-prop engines when on station, and of course they had to pay the 13 men in each crew.

The admiral estimated that pound-for-pound, a few linear inches of a decent LOFARGRAM of this new sub, probably cost the navy half a million bucks. He shrugged as he thought about the other side of the equation too, the people side; the backbreaking work, the lack of sleep, the dangerous crosswinds at Lajes that made every landing a heart-in-your-throat event, and the long times away from families and loved ones. No one could put a dollar value on that. Well, he'd give the analysts as much as they wanted. It was a point of pride with him that his command always came through in the clutch, he was just glad that the weather was holding, the storms of winter made it tough on his men and their machines.

WILSON AND FERNANDEZ TOURED THE ornate palace and found that it really *was* quite beautiful with it's whitewashed exterior walls, it's beautiful mosaics inlaid in many of the interior rooms and the enticingly-beautiful shallow pool in the courtyard. Their guide showed them into the seraglio, where the Bashaw's senior wife had held court over the other 59 junior women. Wilson laughed out loud as their guide tried to hide his embarrassment when she donned one of the traditional veils and acted out her version of assigning the junior women to her "wifely duty watch bill".

"Okay little Najma, you may be a star in the night, but you've got the old geezer from noon 'til supper time; and listen, try and get him to trim back that silly walrus mustache would you? It really bothers the other girls when they're in the clinches with him. Johara, you tiny jewel, you have the evening watch, and not so fast there Hazar; you'll take over for the midwatch, any questions? No? Good, now pass me some more of those delicious dates and my wine glass is almost empty, Fahda you're on wine detail. Ghaliya I see you hiding behind that screen over there, it's your turn to wash my undies, come on *let's GET WITH THE PROGRAM there* ladies!" She'd used her best Master Chief Connolly voice.

Fernandez laughed so hard she had to sit down on the antique divan with it's heap of silk pillows to catch her breath. "Sam I'm glad for the poor old guy, that you weren't in charge of his harem, there would have been a lot fewer children, I'm sure!"

Wilson laughed through the veil, "Maybe so Marty, but I'm sure the old guy would have got his jollies off somehow, my way would have at least made it bearable for the girls, they'd at least have time to get some sleep." She glanced at her wristwatch, "Speaking of time, we've got basketball practice in less than two hours, we'd better get a move on! I'm just glad that Monsieur Madjer's cousin was able to get us this tour."

She took the veil she'd played with and tried to hand it back over to their guide who shook his head and smiled, "Non Mademoiselle please to keeep eet as a geeft, eet ees beeyouteeful on you."

She was charmed, "Merci Monsieur vous êtes très aimable. Quel beau cadeau!" She knew exactly who she would pass the pretty gift on to.

Their favorite taxi driver returned them to the landing and they caught the next launch back to the ship. In their berthing compartment they changed into their shorts and T-shirts, they were ready for practice and had almost a whole hour to spare. Wilson knew how she would fill that time, "Marty I'm heading for the office. I'm going to type a letter to my fiancé and I'll check to see if the boss has any outgoing things. You can come along if you like but I really don't need you, maybe you can go over to *Monty* and see if that cute radioman wants to come and watch us practice."

Fernandez smiled, "Maybe I will Sam, he's more than just cute too, he's nice."

Wilson laughed and grabbed her sweater, she would need it in the office.

Fernandez traipsed off to *Montpelier* and found that RM2 Warner had just finished routing the message boards to the CO, XO and OPS officer. He took the boards back to the radio room to put them away and then he took her to the crew's mess for a snack. The cooks had laid out cookies and brownies and the few crewmen who were relaxing in the mess were writing letters, working on their advancement courses or on watch station quals.

Warner got permission to go watch the women's basketball practice aboard *Ike* with Fernandez. The duty chief allowed it but reminded him that he'd have to hurry back to the boat if there was an emergency called away.

"Don't worry Chief, I'll only be gone for an hour or so, I havta' come back and copy the 1800 broadcast, the captain is anxious to see if there's an update to the LANTINTSUM. I think he has his eye on that new commie submarine the VP guys are all hot and bothered about." He turned to Fernandez, "You've gotta TS clearance don't you Marty?"

She nodded, "Yes Tom, but I don't have any need to know."

He smiled, "That's okay Marty I just didn't want you to be nervous about what we do onboard. Hey lets go see your practice, how many girls will be there anyway?"

She laughed as they headed up the trunk to go topside. "We've got two teams actually, and a total of 21 girls, we just started our league a couple weeks ago, the command master chief is supposed to be getting us real uniforms too. We should be pretty good by the time we get back to Norfolk."

Wilson finished the letter she'd written to Carter and added a few recent snapshots of herself. She gave him a good description of their comic opera and one of the photos was of her in her costume the evening they'd put the show on for the embassy staff. She was sure he would get a kick out of her standing with the admiral during their curtain call.

She locked up and ran down to join the others at practice and saw that Marty had managed to charm the cute radioman into coming to watch them play. In fact there was quite a number of spectators for their practice, she hadn't seem this many before. Ted and Dorothy were sitting in the bleachers too, of course they weren't paying much attention to the players, they were more interested in each other. She wasn't surprised, her favorite couple savored each moment they could be together and she aided and abetted their togetherness as much as she could. After all, it was she who had figured out how to put them together in Ashdod in the first place. Golly they would make a handsome couple when they walked down the aisle together! She hoped she could figure out a way to get to their wedding, if it was in Pasadena it would be a stretch, but she would figure a way, they were her best friends.

The practice turned out to be a good workout and the women felt good about themselves when they finished. Fernandez said goodbye to her admirer but they made plans to watch the movie later in *Montpelier's* crew's mess. She watched him go then, headed back down to his submarine and all the secret things she had heard him talking about with his chief. She knew they did things differently on the submarine than they did here on *Ike*. Intelligence reports were handled by a whole division of operations and intelligence specialists, their "spook shop," within the operations department and they had secure spaces to keep track of everything. She'd had to take something to the captain once when he'd been in there and she had seen the big combination lock on the safe-like door to their spaces. On the sub they just had a radio room and a control room, any incoming intelligence messages had to be handled by the radiomen, quartermasters and the ship's officers. Well she'd have supper with Tom in a little while and watch the movie with him too. She thought he was pretty special, he was the kind of nice man she could take home and introduce to her folks.

Warner flipped on the SSIXS system and made sure it still had the right key card in its crypto "crib" for the day. It would only take a few seconds to copy the 1800 broadcast and then he'd print out the messages on their teletype—TTY—printer. It didn't make much sense to him, the SSIXS could transmit or receive thousands of words a second but after the messages were in its little processor "brain" he could only print them out at less than a hundred words a minute. It didn't matter though he thought, "The captain can only read them just so fast anyway."

Most of the messages were just housekeeping but he had to account for every number on the broadcast. He saw that they already had many of them aboard, they had come in on earlier broadcast "skeds". There were some that were ACTION to other submarines in the Mediterranean and one or two that were only INFO to them. Finally he found what the captain had been looking for, it was a SECRET message from FICLANT that had an updated position on the Soviet sub. The VPs were hot on his trail and it looked like he might pass through the GIUK Gap very soon but where he went after that was anybody's guess.

Warner was about to take the update message to the captain's stateroom when he saw a light flash on the SSIXS control panel. It was a yellow light and it flashed twice quickly before it went out. It meant that the receiver's buffer still had something in it. There was another message to print out. He dumped the buffer and the TTY began it's mechanical chattering at once. The first line of the message's broadcast "header" printed out and his eyes went wide in surprise; FLASH TRAFFIC FOLLOWS, TOP SECRET COWCATCHER CO XO OPS OFFICER EYES ONLY. Warner flipped off the printer and immediately clicked the switch on the 21MC, "Captain to radio!"

He unlocked the door and seconds later the captain and the XO both arrived, the ops officer was only a moment behind them.

Warner pointed to the printer, "Eyes Only Flash ready to dump out of the buffer Captain, just flip the switch there and I'll stand back so you can look it over."

Commander Cushman nodded, "Thanks Petty Officer Warner, go ahead and go on down to the mess, your visitor is there waiting for you, we'll lock up when we're done."

Cushman flipped on the printer and the message printed out one line at a time. It was surely from the highest level in the chain of command, they didn't toss around these "COWCATCHER" things at any of the intermediate level headquarters, Hell there were probably only a handful of people who even knew the code word, let alone what it meant. When the printer stopped, Cushman tore off the yellow sheet and quickly scanned the action order. Then he handed it to the XO.

"Bill let's do a nose count so we can figure out who we still need, but this says we have to leave pretty much pronto to get in position to head off that Type four. I'm going over to *Ike* and talk to the admiral, I'm not sure they sent him a copy of this and I don't want him sandbagged. I'll have to get Chris Christensen's help too. *Ike'll* have to help us get underway. Have the 'chop' figure out if we'll be short anything if we're at sea for a month. My bet is that the slippery serpent is bound for the Med so we'll probably be back here in a few weeks anyway, but who knows."

Warner found Fernandez sitting with a couple of *Ike* sailors waiting for the first sitting for chow. That black guy, Sam Wilson's boxing partner and his girlfriend Judy Obenauf were there to see Ted Manckowicz and of course Dorothy was there with him. He walked in and took the seat next to Marty. The chief cook was almost ready to send out the food. Warner saw the XO headed forward, looking like he was anxious to find someone and at the same time they heard the 1MC's bleat: MONTPELIER DEPARTING! Warner knew it had to be something to do with the 'Eyes Only' message.

He glanced at the others, "Something big is up, the captain just got a flash message with a classification so high I couldn't even look at it, one of those 'burn your eyes out after you read it' messages."

Admiral Townsend was just sitting down in the flag mess to have his supper with the chief of staff, his operations officer and a few others when Commander Cushman knocked and was invited in. "Come on in John, we're just getting started."

He signaled to his Chief MS, "Anselmo, set a place for Captain Cushman please."

Cushman thought about it and knew that it was the right thing to do, Admiral Townsend was a great boss and it was not smart to turn down his offer of a free dinner even though he had burning-hot things to do. He pulled out the chair next to the battle group operations officer and sat down. "Thank you Admiral my business can surely wait until after supper."

Wilson couldn't find her friends at their usual table on the mess decks, "Well maybe they're down on *Montpelier* now, I can't remember what Ted said their menu was for tonight."

She walked to the flight deck and made a bee line to the accommodation ladder and down to *Monty's* deck. TM3 Lupo was standing just aft of the sail and he nodded when she asked him if Judy, Bad Billy or Marty were aboard.

"Yeah Sam, they're all here and Dorothy is too. Hey would you let me have a picture of you in your 'Pinafore uniform'? I got to watch most of the show and I thought it was pretty damn cool!"

Wilson laughed, "Sure Sweetie, I'll send you one in the morning. Can I go down to join them on the mess decks now?"

"Sure Sam, you're always welcome aboard."

She gave him her trademark smile as she crossed the deck and headed down the hatch, on her way to the crew's mess. She arrived at the same time as the XO who greeted her with a smile and then tapped Warner on the shoulder. "I'll have a couple outgoing messages for you to cut as soon as the captain gets back aboard Petty Officer Warner."

Warner was pretty sure those had to do with the flash message the captain had taken with him. Something must really be up. He could almost imagine what would come next and if they ended up snorkeling during the movie he'd know for sure. "Got it XO, you gonna need any of the reference books in radio?"

"Probably, but I'm not sure which ones yet, the navigator is checking that now."

Wilson didn't need to be told that something was up. References stored in the radio room were probably Top Secret, and outgoing messages that needed reference books to write them meant something highly classified, toss in mention of the navigator and it was probably something to do with going somewhere, somewhere secret, somewhere quickly.

Admiral Townsend didn't have the message Cushman had in his pocket and he took it from him, "Let's see what you've got there John."

It only took a moment for him to see what was coming, "This Russian must be really something if they're stealing you away from us. Do you need anything from me before you shove off?"

"No Sir, but I'll stop by and let Chris know we're going and hopefully his bo'sun's mates can help with the line handling. It'll take a couple hours for us to heat up the plant and get self-sustaining but I think we can be underway by just after midnight. I'm doing a headcount now and we'll recall everyone that's ashore, I'll let my visitors stay aboard until we station the maneuvering watch. We'll leave here like thieves in the night. Hopefully we'll snap this Bozo up and keep track of him all the way back here. There's a good chance we'll chop back to you in a week or so. It was great working for you Admiral, we can't wait to get back!"

They rose and shook hands, "Good hunting John, be careful and when it's all over I'd love to hear about it, at least the part that I'm read in for."

"Aye, aye Sir, by the way you make a great Sir Joseph."

Cushman made his way to *Ike's* captain's mess and walked in on the dessert course. Captain Christensen and his XO had been joined by the doctor and some of the COs of their air squadrons.

Christensen invited the sub captain to join them, but he begged off. "Thank you Captain but I can't stay, and I need to ask a favor too; can you have your SPs check around the normal haunts ashore for any of my crew and pass the word there is a recall in progress? We'll get underway just after midnight and I'll need your help there too. We'll keep your shore power until we're self-sustaining."

He knew men from several of Ike's departments would have to scramble to retrieve the heavy cables and help his ship get underway.

Christensen knew that if *Montpelier* was getting underway in the dead of night something serious must be up, "I'll pass the word right away John, will you need a tow to get away from your mooring?"

Cushman wasn't sure, they'd had a tug come and assist when they'd unmoored in the Bay of Palma. "Hopefully no Captain, I can get the stern out and away with my outboard but getting the bow clear may be harder with the currents here."

Christensen thought for a moment, "My gig and the admiral's barge have a little over five hundred horsepower between them, we'll rig a bridle and haul you away from the side. Let me get my first lieutenant on it. If you need anything else my whole crew is here to help."

They had started snorkeling and had stationed the "Condition One" watch in the engineering spaces by the time that Cushman returned to *Montpelier*. His deck force was breaking down the portable jack and flagstaffs and the topside safety lines.

He called for a meeting in the wardroom to take stock of where they were. The COB had the short list of crewmen who were not yet aboard and the navigator had laid out their track to intercept the slithering red menace in the Atlantic. Their onboard stores of food would be enough to last them for a month, any longer than that and they'd be down to the last of the dreaded powdered eggs.

Manckowicz was called away from the crew's mess by the COB, there was a lot to do before they got underway. He gave his beautiful fiancée a kiss and told her he'd be back as soon as he could. She and her girlfriends were still sitting in the mess when IC2 Corday walked in looking for Lupo.

"Anybody seen Lupo?"

Wilson remembered he'd had the topside watch, "I saw him topside when I came aboard."

Corday nodded, "Thanks Sam, I'd better talk to him before things really get out of hand, the idiot lost one of the reels of *Gandhi!*"

CHAPTER 12
DIPLOMACY

WILSON AND HER FRIENDS BADE the *Montpelier* men farewell when the 1MC announcement sent the crew to man their maneuvering watchstations. Bates and Obenauf had already gone by then, Bate's efforts were needed to help get *Monty* underway and Obenauf knew she would just be in the way.

Stanfield stayed of course, she wanted to squeeze out the last moment of the time she'd have together with her big fiancé. He had hurried to remove the ballast tank vent covers and stowed them away so that he could come back and hold her. Wilson was sad to see them go but she knew they were outbound on something important, something special. Even though she might never know what that was, she was excited to be even a tiny part of it. She and Fernandez had listened as Petty Officer Corday had grilled the hapless Lupo. The COB had stepped in to prevent Lupo from having his testicles ripped off and he pleaded with Wilson. "Sam, we don't have the time to try and *unscrew* this up. Is there something you can do to track that reel down? Maybe the embassy can help. You've got another what, two more days here?"

Lupo's story had been that he'd received the box of reels from an ensign who'd said he was from *Porter*. Stanfield knew that it could only have been their new ensign Mr. Nagle and she imparted that to Wilson who reassured the COB.

Wilson figured it out, "Don't worry COB I promise to look into this and figure out what happened."

She gave him her best I've-handled-lots-worse-messes-than-this smile, "I'll get that reel back somehow for you COB, please be careful doing whatever you're doing out there, and I hope to see you soon, back with us."

As they were leaving, Wilson overheard the navigator talking with the chief quartermaster. He said it was about 470 miles to the Strait of Gibraltar and 1500 miles from there. She, Dorothy and Fernandez were the last to leave the boat and they waited on the hangar deck to watch as Bates and his special party idled in alongside *Monty* with the gig and the barge. Manckowicz took the towing bridle they passed to him and made it up to their forward outboard cleat. The linehandlers took in their lines and the two little boats revved their engines and managed to steadily pull her bow out from *Ike's* overhanging side, as her outboard pushed out the stern. It only took a few minutes and they were able to cast off the improvised "tugs" and to thank their creative cox'ns.

Montpelier was underway as her captain had planned, just after midnight. They crept stealthily from the outer harbor and dove as soon as they were past the fifty fathom curve. Then they cranked up their big General Electric main turbines and set a new speed record, racing for the straits and the Atlantic beyond, they would only slow down again when they reached a spot where they could lie in wait for the slippery Soviet sub.

Wilson and Fernandez made their way toward their berthing compartment after they wished Stanfield good night, and she sadly made her way back to *Porter*. Whatever emergency that had caused *Montpelier* to cut short her port visit had robbed her of two more days with her wonderful fiancé. "That was the only problem with the navy," she thought. "Your true love is always in danger of being taken away quickly."

In the morning Wilson checked with the captain and determined that Fernandez could handle the administrative load for the day. She would take the morning and attempt to find the missing movie reel.

She had only one lead, and it seemed to her that she should start by looking at the bitter end of the chain of events that she could only imagine had taken place.

The captain wished her luck in her quest and told her to take along anyone and anything she needed. She thanked him and she was off. She would talk first with the man who had brought the film reels to *Montpelier* and handed them to the luckless Lupo. She had to start with Ensign Nagle. On to *USS Porter*.

Wilson stopped by commander Gavin's cabin and knocked on his door, receiving an "Enter" in a tone of voice that she recognized as: "annoyed".

She pushed open the door and found that he was digging through a stack of paper, looking for something that might help him answer a question about whatever it was he was working on. She put on her most dazzling smile and plowed ahead, "Good morning Commander Gavin I've come to ask for your help in finding the missing reel of *Montpelier's* movie, *Gandhi*, that was shown the other night at the embassy."

Gavin's day took a decided upturn with the arrival of the spritely yeoman. Every interaction he'd ever had with her had been a good one and he wished he had a dozen like her aboard to help him. He got up quickly and held out his hand, "Hello Sam! How can I help? A missing part of a movie can surely screw up a ship's life. A whole reel short?"

"Yes Sir, I think it was probably something that happened at the embassy or possibly along the trail back to the anchorage and *Montpelier* afterwards, I'd like to speak with Mr. Nagle, I understand that he brought a box of film back to the *Montpelier* that night Sir."

Gavin felt a tiny shiver at the base of his spine. Ensign Nagle had only reported aboard the previous week, but already he had shown his spots, he'd managed to drop his plate in the wardroom creating a mess on the deck that the mess attendants had grumbled about to the mess caterer, who had grumbled to the XO, who had brought the clumsiness to his attention.

"Sam why don't you have a seat in my mess and I'll have someone find him."

Wilson thanked him and the captain's mess supervisor made her comfortable there until Gavin ushered the young man in, several minutes later.

She smiled as Commander Gavin motioned for him to take a seat and began the introductions, "Petty Officer Wilson this is Ensign Nagle. Nagle, Miss Wilson is a great friend of the ship and she's looking into something that she thinks you can help with. I'm relieving you of all your other responsibilities for the rest of the day and turning you over to her." He moved to the door and looked back as he opened it and left, so that Wilson could ask her questions.

Wilson thought she saw a look of relief on the commander's face, and then he smiled at her as he closed the door.

Nagle hadn't a clue what was happening, this woman sailor was wearing a third class yeoman's crow on the sleeve of her jumper but she had a Surface Warfare Device above her ribbons and she had three of them He recognized two; the National Defense Service Ribbon and the Navy Commendation Medal, but he wasn't sure of the third. She also had a blue and white ribbon on the right side of her uniform, he'd have to look up what that meant later. She seemed nice enough and the captain obviously knew her and respected her because he had referred to her as "Miss". And of course she was knockout gorgeous too, she was definitely in the same looks category as that knockout gorgeous woman PN he'd turned his service record over to in the ship's office when he'd reported aboard. He cleared his throat and asked, "Ma'am how can I help you today?"

Wilson smiled and giggled inside, this might be harder than she'd thought. "Mr. Nagle please call me Sam and what I need is for you to go over with me what happened the other night when you took the movie back to the *Montpelier*. Could you start at the beginning; and if you don't mind, I'll take notes as we go along."

Nagle blinked and began his description of the evening's events, she had to stop him twice in order to get him to begin at the *real* beginning; watching the embassy's projectionist put the four reels into the cardboard box. He was a little fuzzy on some of the details, especially when it came to remembering the events related to the taxi.

Wilson was patient with the young ensign, asking the pointed questions that led her to the only conclusion she could draw: somehow his clumsiness had resulted in the loss of a reel in the back seat of an Algerian taxicab. "Okay Mr. Nagle can you tell me something about the cab or the driver that will help me find the missing reel?"

Nagle tried to recall, "Well it was blue I think, maybe tan. It was dark so I'm not sure of the color. I know it wasn't an American car, I think it might have been a Peugeot or one of those other French kind. All I remember is that it seemed to rattle a lot and wheeze too."

Wilson thought that was the dumbest thing she'd ever heard, well the dumbest since that fatuous little twit Ruthie Evans had suggested moving Labor Day to March, so she could have her birthday off from school. She focused though, no need letting this young officer know what she thought of his powers of observation.

"What about the driver, what do you remember about him?"

Nagle wrinkled his forehead trying to remember, "Well he seemed twentyish, he had a big black mustache and he could speak a little bit of English."

Wilson knew that most of the taxis in town were French cars and most of those were rattletraps; as far as drivers went, they probably all had black hair and mustaches. Clearly those who wanted to get decent tips had mastered at least a few words in English. Nagle was no help at all there. She had a thought, "Okay Mr. Nagle I'm going to have to do some detective work and I'll have to ask you to come along with me so that perhaps you can identify the driver, after I ask questions ashore. If you could change into your liberty uniform and meet me on *Ike's* quarterdeck in half an hour, we'll go try to track down the missing reel. I have to go find a volunteer to help us, and then I'll meet you there."

She got one of the bo'sun's mates to go check deck division's men's berthing and sure enough Bates was still racked out, sleeping off his late night's work helping their submariner friends get underway. When he heard that Sam had urgent need of him he threw on his uniform and hurried to find her.

Her face lit up when she saw him coming, "Billy I'm sorry I had to wake you up but this is an emergency and I need your help, somehow a reel of *Gandhi* got lost the other night when the movie was being hot reeled. I can trace it until it came time to come back aboard. I'm pretty sure a butterfingered ensign dropped it in the back seat of a taxi. He doesn't remember the cab or the driver but he's willing to go with me and try to identify the driver. I want you to come too. You'll have to take me in the gig and you're my ace in the hole if things get crazy and we have to get physical to get the reel back. Come on, I have to meet that ensign on the quarterdeck in a few minutes."

Nagle was waiting when Wilson and Bates arrived on the quarterdeck and he was even more confused when the woman sailor and her black shipmate asked him to follow as they led him to the boom and waved him into *Eisenhower's* ornate gig. They were underway moments later and Nagle enjoyed the ride as the two sailors conversed quietly by the helm. Certainly this pretty blonde sailor must swing some considerable weight if she could use the gig of the biggest, most powerful ship in the fleet whenever she wanted to. He'd have to check with the senior watch officer and find out the full story about her.

Bates idled in against the landing float and their bowhook quickly made them fast. Wilson led them up to the street level and she made a bee line to the mob of urchins blocking their way to the street. She would enlist their aid, "Bonjour mes enfants, j'ai besoin de votre aide a trouver le chauffer qui à conduit cet officier de l'ambassade il y trois nuits." She turned to Nagle, "I asked them to help us find the driver who brought you here three nights ago."

Nagle had to hand it to her, these kids probably knew every taxi driver in the city and if she could offer a reward for the one who could find him for her, it might just work. In the mean time she would check with their old friend the Sultan of taxi drivers and see if he knew anything. But first she had to find him. "Les enfants, pourriez-vous me montrer où se trouve le taxi de Monsieur Madjer?"

One of the ragamuffins pointed to the street beyond and Wilson quickly led them to the battered Citroen. Nagle had a glimmer of recognition when he saw the car. "This could be the one Miss Wilson! It looks the same but the driver is much older than the man who brought me back to the pier."

Wilson thought it was just too easy that they would discover the missing reel in the first cab they checked, and she was right. Monsieur Madjer would of course be so happy to help le belle mademoiselle but alas he had no knowledge of un bobine de film. However, he would be pleased to convey her concern to his brethren, tout de suite! Within the day he would know of any taxi driver, any chauffeur de taxi, who had any knowledge of this terrible inconvenience to le belle mademoiselle. His brothers, his cousins and his multitude of nephews would most quickly inform the others in his profession and of course if le belle mademoiselle would wish to offer a modest récompense, everything would go so *very much* plus vite!

Wilson knew from her reading of the embassy's briefing papers that any transaction in Algiers would move along much faster if a thing called "baksheesh" was applied to the matter. There was a warning included in the discussion though, which seemed to dissuade any use of this third-world concept, but she knew that if she didn't make it a rewarding experience, the return of the reel would move along at glacial speed. She only had two days to get it back and she knew what to do. "Je l'accepterai comme une faveur si l'homme qui l'a trouvèe s'indentifie. Je ferai de lui un homme très heureux."

The driver's eyes lit up and he thanked her most gratefully adding that he would proceed with all dispatch and get the ball rolling. Bates was curious, "What did you tell him Sam?"

She laughed, "Billy I told him that I would consider it a personal favor if the driver who found the reel would contact me. I told him I would make him a very happy man."

Nagle wondered what it would take to make that happen but he didn't venture an opinion. All he knew for sure was that he was in the presence of a pretty special sailor and he was learning things they hadn't brushed on in OCS or Surface Warfare Officer School. "Excuse me Miss Wilson could you tell me what you want me to do next?"

She wasn't sure that he could be of any value at this point, but she had an idea. "It's Sam please Mr. Nagle, I think we should move the inquiry to the embassy. After that I want to go to a place where the drivers gather for coffee and gossip. I'll find such a place from our friend Monsieur Madjer."

A quick stop at the American embassy revealed that Wilson was on the right track. No one there could recommend contacting the police and making a statement. In fact that would probably be counterproductive because the customary "hand greasing" would take up all available reward money by the time they made the local corporal level happy.

A quick stop at the embassy's money exchange window let her change the dollars she had brought along with her for dinars, and armed with a hefty sheaf of the tissue-paper-like notes, she rejoined Bates and the wretched young officer in the cab.

She knew just what to say, "Grand-père, s'il te plaît amène-nous au lieu préféré des chauffeurs de taxi!"

CHAPTER 13
THE KASBAH

"I ASKED HIM TO TAKE us to the favorite haunt of the taxi drivers, I'm hoping we'll have a good turnout. I think that Monsieur Madjer may be to the local taxi profession, what Master Chief Connolly is to all our shipmates on *Ike*. We'll spend the rest of the morning there and see what turns up. If we hear nothing, then we'll have to revise the plan."

Bates thought it was a genius idea and the nascent ensign didn't know what to think, he had been pretty much in a fog since the XO had grabbed him out of the wardroom and sent him to report to the captain earlier that morning.

Their driver placed his machine in gear and left the embassy behind, bound for the popular hangout that housed both a café and a hookah parlor. After a series of known-only-to-him turns he pulled onto Ahmed Bourzina St. and increased speed bound for the Kasbah. He drove along, happy to be at the nexus of this intrigue; the très belle mademoiselle seemed to be quite intent on finding this bit of American foolishness. If he could be of assistance, he might gain preferred status with the diplomats at their embassy. He might also recover a goodly fee from the driver who would come forward for the reward.

He already knew where the errant reel of film resided. It had found its way to the usual place where ill-gotten items went; the thieves market, the stalls and shops just outside the Kasbah in the old city. He only needed to determine from his serpentine network of contacts who the very fortunate finder had been. Then it was only a matter of convincing that driver to come and present himself with the purloined reel and accept the profound thanks of the Americans … and of course the big roll of bills that he had seen the grande blonde beauté pass to her ebony compatriot when they had exited from the embassy.

Bates was watching their journey carefully, his natural habit of observing, assessing and remembering the route. He could memorize the names on the shops and the street names they crossed just like he could gauge the distance from the bow of his small boat to the pier, even in heavy rain or fog. "Sam I don't know where we're going but I'll know how to get back."

She had confidence in her friend, he was the epitome of a sailor in her eyes; physically superb and totally a shipmate. Bad Billy Bates was her best friend and he had helped her in so many ways, so often and so completely that he was *more* than just a shipmate, he was a big brother. Just as Shakespeare had written and Nelson had stressed in talking with his captains before the Battle of the Nile. Wilson felt the tingles in her tummy that she always felt when it came time to do her duty, in whatever task she was called on to perform. She was sure that her friend would have her back in any decision she made.

"Billy, it's okay, I'm thinking that we'll be able to take advantage of the goodwill that our being here has caused and maybe we'll get lucky. The drivers have hauled a lot of sailors around the city and they'll want those fares and tips to continue when the next group of sixth fleet ships comes to visit here. I hope this place he's taking us to has some decent food. Billy I'm sorry for breaking you out of your bunk, guess what, I'll buy you some lunch, and you can try your best to punch my lights out this evening," she gave him her best sly-little-pout smile and batted her lashes at him. "Then we'll call it even okay?"

Bate's smile spread over his face like a sunny day, "Sam you know I'd get up and help you no matter when or what for. I think it's my turn to buy you lunch and as for punching, hey the last time we got in the ring together you almost wore me out."

She laughed and turned to Nagle, "Sir Petty Officer Bates is my boxing instructor and he's my best friend, he doesn't really punch me out."

Nagle was now totally confused but he smiled and nodded as if sailors making small talk about beating each other up was something that he witnessed every day.

Their resourceful driver turned off the broad thoroughfare and into a narrow alley lined on each side with seedy looking shops and bars. Bates noted that they had turned north, toward the sea, they must be nearing the Kasbah now. A few moments later they emerged from the dark alley onto Rue Saadi et Mokhtar Hafidh. It was one of the streets that the embassy had listed in their briefing papers as an area to stay away from. Wilson was glad she had her best friend along with her.

Their unerring driver pulled into a sizeable parking area in front of a wide sandstone building with a dark, wooden entry door and a portico with benches under the overhanging roof. A small group of men dressed in an assortment of European clothes and Arab robes sat on the benches having Turkish coffee and sharing the news and gossip of the day. A dozen other taxis were already parked out front and as they were climbing out of their car another one pulled in behind them.

Their obliging driver led them to the door and pushed it open, inviting the sailors to follow him inside. It was a low-ceilinged room with round pillars on either side of a wide passageway. Sofas lined the right wall where curtains could be drawn to allow the men privacy as they smoked their hookahs and gambled or played dominoes. Alcoves along the left wall sectioned the café part of the establishment into small family-sized compartments for eating. The kitchen and a bar occupied the back of the building. It was noisy and boisterous and Wilson thought it was a lot like visiting the set of an old movie about the French Foreign Legion. She could imagine young women belly dancing to entertain the men. She could also see that she was the only woman in the room.

Their august driver invited them to sit at a table in one of the alcoves and waved for a waiter to come and take their orders while he went to converse with his esteemed compatriots in the hookah section. A waiter appeared and handed them a menu of the day's offerings. Wilson nodded and ordered for them, "Des bière pour mes amis s'il vous plaît, et un thé pour moi."

The waiter smiled through his whiskers and nodded, disappearing soundlessly to reappear moments later with two French beer bottles, "*Castelains*", and a pot of tea, cream and sugar with their glasses and Wilson's cup on his tray. Wilson thanked him and pointed to her companions, "S'il vous plaît, Monsieur, le ragoût de poulet pour trois."

The waiter nodded and disappeared again returning shortly with a large square of flatbread and three large bowls. A kitchen helper followed with a serving dish full of couscous and a big earthenware pot. Wilson thought it looked like her mom's big rumtopf pot as the helper set it down on their table and served the steaming-hot contents into their bowls. They took their spoons and tasted the kitchen's offering finding it savory and delicious. There were many different vegetables and big chunks of the delicious chicken floating in a thick cream-colored sauce. Bates had to admit that it was the finest chicken stew he had ever tasted, The ensign was impressed with it too, and he could eat as much of it as he wanted and not have to wait to be served until all the senior officers had gotten theirs. The waiter and his kitchen assistant stood by unobtrusively as they ate their first bowlfuls and filled them again as soon as they were empty. It was simple food but wholesome and incredibly delightful.

Wilson kept listening attentively, attuned to the murmuring chatter of the men coming from the other side of the room, behind the beaded curtains in the hookah parlor. From time-to-time one or two of them would emerge, leaving their smoke, to depart through the front door. They would be replaced, in turn, by new arrivals who had finished their taxi runs or had just stopped by for their normal, early afternoon respites. She was convinced that the message was being disseminated to the taxi driver community by the departing men just as surely as the word would get out to every man and woman on *Ike*, as a result of attending morning quarters. Of course the navy way was much faster.

They finished their lunch and Wilson asked the waiter if there was a restroom. She had a feeling that whatever facilities there were would probably not be up to the standards of the navy. Bates read her mind, "Sam I'll go first and check it out."

The waiter took him to the back door and pointed to the small detached outbuilding behind the kitchen. Bates went in and found it to contain a wash basin with a faucet. There was no toilet though, only a hole in the tile floor where apparently one did one's business. There was no toilet paper available either. He made the best of it and headed back inside. "Sam it's a hole in the floor, you can't sit down and there's no toilet paper."

"Is there any water Billy?"

"Yes there's a working sink but no hot water and no hand towels."

Wilson shivered as she thought about it, but it wouldn't be the first time she'd have to pee standing up. The 'women's head' was just a patch of sand behind a broken boulder and a driftwood tree trunk when she'd been marooned with the others in the little cove on the island of Capri, back in May.

"Thanks Billy, I've come prepared."

She opened her purse and pulled out a few sheets of Kleenex, it would double as toilet tissue and hand towels. Bates showed her the way and went back to their table.

Ensign Nagle was curious, "Who is that woman anyway?"

Bates grinned as he laughed softly, "That, Mr. Nagle, is the finest sailor in the United States Navy, she's a friend and shipmate to everybody and believe me if she says she's gonna get that movie reel back she's gonna do it."

Nagle was still a bit foggy, "But she's a third class petty officer, how come she's in charge of a second class and an officer?"

"You must be really new Sir. If you had been with us a few weeks ago when we made our combined port visit in Mallorca, you'd have watched her get that Navy Commendation and that Navy Marine Corps Medal. You would have heard the fleet commander say how great she is in front of every sailor on *Porter*, *Montpelier* and *Ike*. Some day when you can sit down with your captain, ask him why he has that picture on his desk of her with the two admirals. Believe me you'll never meet anyone like her again. Here she comes now. Don't let her see we were talkin' about her."

Wilson returned to their table and took her seat, "Well that's not something I'm going to put in my next letter home Billy!" She shivered in disgust, "That smelled even worse than that French ship. That was *really* icky."

Bates nodded as the young officer got up to take his turn at a head call. While he was gone their driver emerged from the hookah section with the news that another driver had been located who might know something about the missing spool of film. He worked the evening shift but he would make his way to them by late afternoon.

Wilson was hopeful, "Excellent mon ami! Est-ce qu'il apportera la bobine avec lui?"

She turned to Bates, "Our friend says the driver who found the reel will be here later this afternoon. I asked if he'd bring the reel."

By the time Nagle returned, their driver had verified that the errant reel would indeed be in the hands of the much anticipated driver and they settled in to wait. Wilson ordered the men another round of the French beer and she got herself a Turkish coffee. She thought that the strong taste might help chase away the last lingering trace of latrine odor from her nose and mouth.

It was almost dusk when the driver finally came in with the reel. Monsieur Madjer brought him to their table and he made a courteous bow to Wilson but kept a tight hold on the reel. Nagle recognized him right away.

"Sam that's him, the driver who picked me up at the embassy!"

Wilson acknowledged him, "Thank you Mr. Nagle now we need to make him part with that reel and give it to us. I'm going to try negotiating with him."

She hoped her little French would be enough to convince him to part with the reel and let her take it back to her ship. If she was successful she would then have to figure out how to get it back to *Montpelier*. She wondered which part would be harder.

CHAPTER 14
FATE INTERVENES

MONSIEUR MADJER MADE APOLOGIES TO Wilson and provided the last snippet of information that would enable her to convince the driver to hand over the reel. The driver was one of his ubiquitous and seemingly numberless band of nephews, Wajid, the sixth son of his youngest brother Achmed.

Wilson stood and took the hand of the newly-arrived benefactor and noted the resemblance, younger by far, but with the same nose and a much blacker mustache. She hoped her idea would work, "Bonsoir Monsieur. L'once Mustafa m'a dit que vous pourriez m'aider à résoudre un petit probléme et rendre une bobine à mes supérieurs de la marine."

The younger driver engaged his uncle in a loquacious discussion intermixed with much shrugging and hand gesticulation which lasted until Wilson nodded to Bates, her signal for him to pull the enticing roll of dinars from his pocket. A mere glance at the money was the final piece of weight that tipped the scale. His uncle's assurance that he would occupy most-favored-driver status with the Americans at the embassy and that the next group of American ships would arrive clamoring for Wajid to carry them all over the city, were both great enticements already. With that kind of increase in his business he could even afford a larger house and add a few more wives to his ever-expanding assortment. If only he could find one a tenth as lovely as this tall, intelligent, beautiful young woman who had managed to find him and had so obviously enraptured his uncle.

Wilson told her companions that she had asked him to help her correct a terrible error and return the reel to her navy superiors. "Mr. Nagle I think when he saw you he knew that we knew we had the right man. When we leave I want you to thank him for helping us too."

Nagle understood, "I caused this whole thing Sam, I feel terrible about it."

She patted his shoulder, "It's okay Sir, we have it now, they'll give us a ride back to the landing and we'll be aboard in time for supper. I'll tell your CO how much I appreciate your assistance and that I personally will contact *Montpelier* and let them know we've got it and will get it to them."

Nagle felt like a million dollars, this was the first time since he'd been in the navy that *anyone* had told him he had been helpful.

Wilson smiled and nodded to Bates who passed the sheaf of notes to the salivating Majid. He stuffed them into the folds of his robe without even counting it and passed the reel to Bates. He pulled out the leader and noted the marking pen scribbles: GANDHI REEL III OF IV. "Got it Sam, this is the real thing, I think we're ready to go. We'd better settle up with the waiter and then we're out of here."

"Thanks Billy, I'm sorry I put every dinar I had into the reward, I hope you can cover the lunch and I promise to make it right next payday."

Nagle wouldn't hear of it, "It's on me Sam, let me make it up to you and Billy okay?"

Here was Nagle springing for drinks again, but this time it was coming out of his wallet.

The happy driver and his venerable uncle had a discussion in Arabic that they couldn't understand but was apparently about who was going to return the group to the port.

Wilson breathed a sigh of relief when they climbed into the gig and Bates fired up the engine. The boat engineer and the bowhook had alternated napping for the lion's share of the day but they looked smart when Sam and that ensign from *Montpelier* stepped aboard. They knew that Bates would exact a stern punishment if they didn't. When they got underway for the boom it was the end of a light day for them but for their passengers it had been long and hard.

Wilson followed the ensign up the boarding ladder and saluted the OOD. She turned to Bates when he arrived there, "Billy could you take the reel to my office and if it's locked leave it with Petty Officer Sims in the pantry, if Marty is still there tell her I'll be there as soon as I pay my respects to *Porter's* CO. After that I'd sure like to have supper with you on the mess decks and then we can find something to do after that."

Bates nodded and smiled his toothy smile at his friend, "Yes Ma'am I'm on it and I'll meet you on the mess decks."

Before she let him go she grabbed the black sailor and hugged him whispering her thanks for helping her and having her back … like he always had.

Nagle watched the exchange and was even more confused. He had to find out how this woman sailor and her black shipmate could do such an un-navy thing as to exchange a hug on the quarterdeck of the biggest, most powerful ship in the navy. He fell in step with her as she led him to the ladder down to *Porter*, "Sam could you clear something up for me?"

She stopped and turned to him, "Of course Sir, what would you like to know?"

"Well, you and Bates seem to be almost a couple I mean are you and he … ?"

She knew what he was asking, "It's not what you think Sir, I'm engaged to a wonderful sailor who just left the battle group to attend Annapolis. Billy is my shipmate. He's been there to help me every time I've needed it and I think of him as a mentor, a teacher, and a brother. I'm an only child, but if I ever had a big or little brother I would want him to be just what Bad Billy is to me. Maybe I shouldn't have hugged him on the quarterdeck, but if you can find an order or a regulation anywhere, against a sister hugging her brother shipboard, I'd really like to see it."

Nagle smiled, "Thank you Sam, I guess I understand."

She laughed, "Good Sir, now let's go find your CO and I'll tell him what a great help you've been today!"

Nagle thought that it was the best lesson he'd ever learned since he'd put on his uniform.

Afterwards Wilson raced to her berthing compartment and stripped off her whites. God that shower felt *so* good! She'd recoiled in horror from the evil disgusting smell in that horrid outhouse but now she knew she could make it. She'd send her uniform to the laundry and hope that Pam and the others there could make it snowy fresh again. Thank goodness they were shifting to blues tomorrow before they got underway.

Wilson needed to do two things before she met Bates and her friends on the mess decks. She'd have to check with the captain and get him caught up on all the mail and she'd let *Montpelier* know that she'd kept her promise to the COB. She knew the captain would help her with that.

"CONN, RADIO, ALL TRAFFIC'S ON board ready to go deep!" Warner flipped the switch on the antenna control panel and the mast slid home inside the sail. He heard the OOD's response on the 21MC and he could feel the hull taking a down angle and the rocking motion of the waves up in the sea state ceased as *Montpelier* sped back down to her transit depth. It had only taken a few minutes, they were on the longest allowed broadcast routine and only had to clear their traffic once every 24 hours. The watch officers at ComSubLant would make sure to minimize their traffic, no one wanted to slow them down as they raced northward to set up their barrier for the Russian sub, only essential messages would appear on their "sked".

Warner dumped the buffer and printed it out on the teletype printer as a single continuous sheet of buff-yellow paper. Afterward he took a metal straightedge and used it to tear the broadcast sheet into its individual messages. Nothing earthshaking he thought, all the top secret stuff had already been cleared by the time they'd reached the Straits of Gibraltar and screeched out into the Atlantic. He'd logged all those COWCATCHER messages and put them on a special message board, then the ops officer had him make up a special top secret sheet that listed every snippet of noise information that their VP brethren had milked from their round-the-clock tracking of the shifty Soviet sub. Sonar would use that as a quick reference.

He scanned the messages before putting them on the boards for routing; only five this broadcast, three PRIORITY confidential ones, something about water chemistry and lube oil, one with some nebulous info about torpedo parts and two PRIORITY unclassified ones: an ALLFOODACT, something about getting rid of certain lots of lima beans and finally a PERSONAL FOR, Holy Smoke! It was from *Eisenhower* and it was for the COB!

PRIORITY
301959Z SEP 83
FM: USS DWIGHT D EISENHOWER CVN 69
TO: USS MONTPELIER SSN 765
INFO: CTG 60.2, USS PORTER DDG 78, AMEMB ALGIERS
UNCLAS //N17101//
SUBJ: LOST FILM REEL

    PERSONAL FOR CHIEF OF THE BOAT

    1. REEL RECOVERED IN ALGIERS EARLIER TODAY.
    2. CURRENTLY IN SAFEKEEPING ABOARD.
    3. PLS TELL LUPO HE OWES ME BIG TIME. HI TO ALL!

HOPE TO SEE EVERYONE IN ROTA! SAM SENDS.
BT

Warner took the message boards to the conn where the OOD initialed them before he took them down to the wardroom. Commander Cushman read the featured message and sent for the COB who arrived a few moments later. "Well COB this one's for you."

The COB read it and smiled, "Cap'n I told you that women sailors would be good aboard the boats and we found out I was right when we had Dorothy and Sam aboard. Now I'm gonna make a prediction, Sam Wilson's gonna be an admiral someday, someday soon!"

Cushman chuckled, "I agree with you COB, you shoulda seen her with that *Pinafore* bunch on the flagship that night. Anybody who can put together a show and have it come out like that in just a few weeks is a force to be reckoned with."

The COB acknowledged the captain's wisdom, "I knew she was something special when I first set eyes on her Cap'n. Well I guess I'd better go find Lupo and tell him his balls are safe, at least for now."

Lieutenant Jaygee Leech spoke up then, "Hey COB, when you run into MM2 Crandall, tell him that his hare-brained idea will not be held against him when I write his next evaluation."

He meant it in jest of course, but the XO didn't; when he added that Leech's next fitness report would certainly reflect his association with the debacle, when he wrote that.

The navigator called down to the wardroom as the COB was leaving, "Cap'n, Navigator; we're in prime position to begin our barrier search for the Type four. Slowing to start the drift phase of our search."

★ ★ ★ ★

WILSON WAS SITTING IN HER normal spot, between Fernandez and the XO, the morning before they got underway. The department heads began arriving soon after she took her seat. Captain Sweeney, the air officer, greeted her, "Good morning Sam, I understand that you were the one who helped one of my petty officers start the ball rolling on the paperwork for her seaman-to-admiral application."

Wilson smiled, "Oh yes Sir, Stef Turner! I think she's a fine sailor, she's one of the mainstays on our woman's basketball team and she's one of Sir Joseph's aunts! Believe me Captain she'll be a dynamite officer. Did you get a chance to interview her yet?"

Sweeney laughed, "Yes I did Sam, just yesterday and I think you're right, she has a great attitude and she's got a good reputation in the department. So what did she have to give up in order to enlist your help getting going on it Sam?"

She giggled, "Well I did get a ride on one of the aircraft elevators. Oh and I got to ride on one of your tractors!"

Captain Christensen started the meeting then and thanked everyone for being there, "Thank you all for being prompt and also thank you for a well conducted port visit. He turned to the first lieutenant, "Dick your folks did really well the other night when we had to help *Montpelier* get to sea."

He turned to Commander Ackman, "Engineer your people did well too, wrestling those heavy cables in the dead of night was hard and dangerous work and your troops did super. Let me know who was involved and we'll talk commendations for them."

Wilson nudged Fernandez and whispered, "Get the list from the engineer officer and then ask the captain if he wants letters of commendation or medals. We should get started on it right after we secure from the special sea and anchor detail." She didn't have to ask the first lieutenant for the list of his people, she would get that from Bad Billy later on.

The department heads all made their reports and Fernandez took down all the details on her pad. Wilson knew she was proficient enough with her shorthand now and she wouldn't miss anything. She was picking up a lot of the specialized jargon of the specific departments too. Wilson was very pleased with her learning speed. She thought Marty would be ready to take the whole load from her before they started their sprint from Rota Spain across the Atlantic to Norfolk.

She had looked over the records of every one of their new-arrival graduates of Yeoman A-school before she had talked with the admin officer. She knew exactly how the captain liked to do the correspondence and how he expected her to help out across the board. Most importantly though, she knew the mood that he liked her to set in the meetings. She had trained Marty well and was sure she could handle it. Her view was that the captain's yeoman was a full-fledged member of the captain's staff and on equal footing with his mess supervisor, the command master chief, the navigator and the XO. Of course the others all got paid a lot more.

The department heads all got up and filed out of the mess headed for their individual duties, there were a million things to do before the most powerful ship in the navy could get underway. Wilson thanked the captain for his help the previous day, "Boss I really appreciate your help on that movie reel thing. I was actually a little scared when the driver took us to that section of town but it turned out okay. I took Billy Bates with me for protection and I grabbed the ensign from *Porter* who could identify the driver and all it cost me was fifty dollars in reward dinars. Oh and thank you for letting me draft that message. I'd never done a message before."

The XO chuckled, "You spent fifty bucks of your own money to get a movie reel back Sam? That's over and above if you ask me!"

She giggled, "Don't worry XO, I'll make sure I get it back after I talk with the COB on *Montpelier*. He'll probably take up a collection to help me out."

The captain smiled then, "Don't worry Sam I'm having *Porter's* CO for lunch before we set the special sea and anchor detail. I'm sure he'll want to share in the pain."

Wilson let Fernandez handle the notes from the captain's meeting as she got to work on the recommendation letter for her friend's application for the seaman-to-admiral program. If she could get that drafted and approved before lunch she could have the whole package in the mail and off the ship via the first COD flight that afternoon.

They had a whole stack of outgoing mail ready to go including the thank you letters to the embassy staff and the Algerian officials who had been instrumental in making the port visit for *Ike* and her battle group mates such a success. She was sure there were bags of official mail ready to send out from the ship's office too, the dull and dreary stuff she dreaded.

"Okay Marty go ahead and start your notes workup, but when you finish with the air and engineering departments let me cut in line for the mag card machine and you can start cranking out copies for the big departments while I run up my recommendation letter. I'll have to take that to the boss and then I'll come help with the rest of the departments. We should be finished with plenty of time to spare. Gosh it's great being back in our blues again isn't it?"

Fernandez agreed, putting on her blues seemed like a signal that they were almost done with their deployment. They only had the two weeks of October to go before they would start winding down their operations and head toward Rota Spain to begin the turn over to the *"Indy"* battle group. She'd enjoy wearing them on the bridge later too, when Sam showed her the ropes and how to help the captain when they got underway. Now *that* was something they had never talked about in yeoman A-school!

CHAPTER 15
UNDERWAY AGAIN

"WARDROOM CONN, SUBMERGED NOISE LEVEL bearing zero, zero five attempting to classify now." Commander Cushman glanced at the wardroom gyro repeater and saw that it confirmed what his senses told him, the ship was turning to the right, putting the unknown noise source across the line of sight and into their port quarter. The conning officer was doing it just right, trying to generate some speed across the line of sight to the newly-gained contact, and trying to minimize the closure rate while they worked to figure out what the noise source was.

They had all the results of the VP's prosecution of the new submarine by message and there were precious few aural clues, so far it was just a little broadband noise with accompanying biologics. Apparently the Russki submarine builders had done a lot of work in making this new guy hard to hear and hard to find, but there was that one tell-tale sound that the LOFAR systems had been able to exploit; and where there was one, Cushman knew there had to be others. The whole reason they had sent his ship on this no-notice mission was to find out what those were, and how to use them against it.

They had run hard, fast and deep, as they had cranked out the miles headed north to the intercept point they had worked out before they'd slipped their mooring and crept out of Algiers. They had raced west and glided out through the narrows that the Straights of Gibraltar made. He'd kept them deep and out of the way of the multitude of commercial shipping that was constantly passing through there, always heavy and headed east or west in almost endless profusion. They'd cleared all their numbered broadcast traffic using their SSIXS system, popping up to snatch a quick dump from the satellite and immediately heading back to their transit depth. They wasted no time getting back to the deep zone and cranking open the throttles.

They'd run for almost three days, as fast as they could go. Thank goodness for Admiral Rickover and his "rocket", they had caught this first sniff of the Russki "badass" just about dead on where they'd figured they might pick him up.

Cushman hit the button on his 21MC handset. "Conn captain aye. Station the tracking party and let me know when we pick up the first confirming 'thumbprint' noise."

"Captain, conn aye."

Cushman knew the navigator was on it and that he had already called away the tracking team. Here was the messenger of the watch to grab the engineer and the three lieutenants who would supervise the plotting and tracking, and tweak the fire control computer for the best solution. Once they'd actually found him they'd crank out a plan to map his noise sources; to work him, and study him, and exploit all his vulnerabilities … if he had any.

He and the XO would spell each other overseeing the actions of the ship and the tracking party. They would make the tough calls and keep track of ship's safety and the big picture. This was the first real opportunity that a US submarine had to work this new class of Russian submarine, to take the measure of this state-of-the-art output of the Soviet peoples' lavishly-funded submarine design and construction program. Cushman thought it would be a chance to determine whether they'd invested wisely or if they'd dumped rubles into a sinkhole that gobbled up a significant chunk of the peoples' treasury and flushed out a turd. Maybe that's the scale he'd apply to the sub in his wrap-up report of the mission, when he went to Washington to debrief it. He'd call it his "turkey-to-bird" ratio and he'd substitute turd for turkey.

It didn't take all that long for the Russki rogue to show up on their digital sonar screens and their sonar team gained familiarity with him quickly. They built a chart of all the different noises that came out of his power plant and his auxiliary machinery. They were even able to draw upon their knowledge of Soviet sub tactical doctrine to build a credible picture of its crew, it's leaders, and their habits. When and how did they do things like: charge their air banks, pump their bilges or flush their heads? They were interested in their tactical savvy too, when and how did they do sonar sweeps to check for those decadent, pesky and persistent, capitalist submarines? When that picture was painted they moved in a little closer.

They heard the bread machine clonking away making the dough for the pirozhki and they heard the screeching of their steam kettle bubbling up the borsht. So much for their breakfast and lunch courses, perhaps they would try something quieter for dinner.

Hour after hour, day after day *Montpelier* tagged along as the uninvited guest of the pest, staying just far enough away to remain undetected. The track took them toward the Mediterranean at a leisurely pace. Clearly the Pride of Polyarny was not in any hurry to get anywhere special. *Monty's* crew began taking bets on the vodka-quaffer's final destination, half seemed convinced that they would truck on in to Alexandria and the other half were sure they would never be able to navigate anywhere nearly as far. They settled on the Gulf of Sidra, the bay off Libya, where the beat-up "Ugra"-class sub-tender had taken station and would serve any Russian submarine who could find it in its lonely anchorage.

It was rumored that they had women aboard their tender too but surely their Katrinkas and Svetlanas weren't anywhere near the caliber of the American women sailors they'd been fortunate enough to befriend on this Med run, and by no stretch of the imagination could they be as brave and beautiful as Manckowicz's delightful Dorothy or as comely and clever as everyone's favorite sweetheart Sam.

Lupo summed it up for most of them when he told the COB that if he had the choice between a wild roll in his rack with a Slavic sailor, or groveling at the feet of Sam Wilson he'd settle for rug burns on his forehead for the rest of his life. The COB wrote that sentiment down in his little book, he'd use it when he wrote his memoirs.

By the time they were lined up to follow Polyarny Piotr through the Straits of Gibraltar, *Monty* had squeezed the dopey drone for every piece of acoustic information she could. It wasn't that the redolent red's equipment wasn't up to standards, they had clearly done much at the shipyard to make it a better boat, it was more a matter of ineptitude. Maybe their whole crew weren't *all* clumsy clowns or butter-fingered buffoons, but they seemed to make un-submariner mistakes all the time. When they blew sanitary tanks it was like sounding a hunting horn they were so unconscious of their air use. They couldn't maintain depth and when they went shallow to communicate or get a fix, they would broach and flail along on the surface. Then they would overcompensate and plummet like a stone only to have to blow ballast, to keep from bonking off the bottom ... or worse. It seemed that the crew couldn't move from one room to another without clanging the doors behind them and their mechanics and torpedo technicians must have been issued the slipperiest tools in the Soviet supply system. Hey every crew had it's one or two dipsticks, *Monty* had Lupo for goodness sake, but a *whole crew* of them? Maybe their draft induction center had been staffed by Larryovsky, Moeskaya and Curlyvitch. For whatever reason, they were laughable.

Commander Cushman asked his team to gather up all the data and all their observations into a nice tight report that he could deliver to the powers that be. He broke it into two sections; the first was a compendium of the comments and observations related to the new sub. It would accompany the reels and reels of acoustic tape they'd recorded. The second was his assessment of its crew and their state of training. The danger was that if some unlikely event caused the crew to become *competent* submariners all of a sudden, the boat would become very hard to find. The chance that they were being played seemed remote, but what if they *were* being played? What if this had all been an expensive and elaborate ruse?

Maybe *Monty* had been detected right at the start and this whole transit to the Med was just a freak show put on by a bunch of crack submariners who were just waiting for the appropriate moment to take off their big red noses and clown suits, slip out of their big floppy shoes and put away their shaving cream pies and seltzer bottles. What if they were all having the horse laugh on them at this very moment?

Cushman got his top talent together to wrestle with that possibility. The XO, navigator, the COB and the weapons officer. He tasked them to come up with a scenario that would help them determine if their nemesis was a maestro or a misfit. Whatever they could cook up they would try, if it made sense to him and it didn't put *Montpelier* or any other US ship in danger.

He gave them the wardroom for the rest of the afternoon and left them alone. He would return when they had their ideas jotted down on a flip chart.

When the XO came to get him he was just finishing his review of the write up of last week's port visit. Damn he had seen how Chris Christensen did his correspondence and he was as jealous as he'd been when he was in the fourth grade and lost two whole bags of marbles to Lester Ewert, now *there* was a marble shooter! Chris had forty times the correspondence that he had, but he had a secret weapon to handle it all. He had the best woman sailor in the fleet and she *could* do it all. Oh well, where had he put that thesaurus anyway?

They brought him back into the wardroom and he sat down to look over the list they had made.

1. Dangle tempting morsel, watch reaction.

2. Follow to port visit, see for ourselves.
3. Hammer with active sonar, watch reaction.
4. Send him a message.
5. Have someone call him "from home".

Cushman thought that the morsel idea was outside the realm of possibility, he'd have to have something really juicy and he'd have to have somebody buy off on it at the JCS level. That was probably a non-starter. To sneak in to their anchorage was doable of course but he'd need JCS buy in there too. Active sonar was easy and so was sending him a message, underwater telephone would work just fine, but he could pretend he hadn't heard it, maybe fake that their sonars weren't working. The one that was intriguing was the last one, have him get a call from "home". But how to make that happen?

Cushman cleared his throat, "Nav what info do we have on ASW flights here outside the Med and what do we know of Soviet surface units that are either in the area or inside the Med?"

"We've got the LANTINTSUMs Captain and we could pop up there and copy the Med sub broadcast, that would give us both the Soviet surface ship activity and the scheduled VP flight data."

"Good, let's do that and we'll see what we have to work with. If we can get an AGI or some other surface guy to be near enough to see what's going on, we could have a VP come in and pound him with active sonobuoys. The word would be shot back to Moscow and they'd have to send his ass a message. In any case we'd know, it's your numbers 3, 4 and 5 all together."

They hauled off a short way and quickly grabbed the Med SSIXS downloads. Cushman had the info he needed and they laid everything out on a chart twenty minutes later. It was a stretch, but there was a way to do it, only he'd need just a little bit of help and the guy who had the assets to help him was the *only* guy in the Med who knew what *Monty* was up to.

"Nav give me the distance to this point in the Balearic Basin and the ETA there assuming a six knot SOA, "Pete" doesn't move much faster than that." He made a dot with his pencil and labeled it "POINT BOZO". "I'm going to write up a message to an old friend, and we'll be sending it off just as soon as this moron were following heads up to get his evening fix."

WILSON HAD EVERYONE IN THEIR costumes walking through a rehearsal the evening after they had gotten underway from Algiers. It was clear that some of the polish they'd had the night they'd put on the show for the embassy staff had tarnished, thank goodness there were another eight days before they were slated to head for Rota.

It was the aunts, they just weren't as sharp as they had been that night, six days ago. "Okay everybody, that's a *wrap* for tonight! Stef can you hold the other aunts up for a minute while I talk with Sir Joseph?"

Turner and her five "sister aunts" huddled at the foot of the stage while the tall blonde sailor conferred with her most senior cast member. "I'm sorry Admiral, we all should have been more ready tonight, but I promise, we'll be *sparkling* tomorrow."

He chuckled as he squeezed her shoulder, "It's okay Sam, don't worry we still have plenty of time. We'll nail it tomorrow I'm sure."

He headed off to the flag spaces then, Wilson knew he probably had a ton of work to catch up on. He'd left her feeling better though, but she knew she'd have to slip in an extra rehearsal, and that would cut into the cast's time off from their normal duties. It was funny, she thought of the others as "her" cast members rather than as *Ike* crew members, officers and petty officers from their air squadrons or as members of the flag staff. Already the flag secretary was starting to look a bit frazzled, her normal work with the admiral's staff took up most of her day and leading the orchestra was a big slice of her evening. Wilson was worried that she was working them all too hard.

During rehearsal they'd had to contend with the normal work of the ship, performing her mission, conducting flight ops. The noise of the landings, as the A6s and F14s trapped on the flight deck above them, was more than just a little bit distracting. The screaming of the jet engines and the thumping, jarring, heavy sound of the planes' wheels whamming down on the deck followed by the sharp sound of the arresting cables as they tensed under the strain. Then after a pause to unhook and move the plane, the prolonged dragging sound as the heavy cables were hauled back into position for the next landing. She relented, with all that going on it was a wonder the aunts had been able to concentrate at all.

"Alright ladies was there a problem or was it just me that noticed you were late coming in during Sir Joseph's *Monarch of the Seas* number?"

Turner knew she was right, "Yes Sam, and it was all my fault, every time I hear one of those cables rattle and scrape I just think about the poor pilot if the thing snaps and he splashes into the ocean right in front of us and we're barreling along so fast we'd just plow him deeper into the sea. I apologize and I'll try to do better. It's not Sara or the others it's me."

Wilson saw that she had a tear forming in the corner of her right eye and she reached out with both arms to embrace her friend. "Stef it's fine, it was just a little timing glitch and the real fault is mine, I should have held the rehearsal in the crew's lounge instead of here on the set, I didn't give the flight ops a thought. I'm sorry Stef, please don't cry."

Turner hugged her back and calmed down again, as far as she was concerned, if Sam said it would be okay, it *would be* okay.

Admiral Townsend was very busy after the rehearsal was over. His communications watch officer had presented him with an EYES ONLY message from *Montpelier* that had been double encrypted.

That meant that it had a TO and a FROM line on the normal encrypted fleet broadcast, but the body of the message looked like gobbledygook to every other broadcast recipient except for the one it was intended for. That recipient had to take the message and pull out a special code book so he could break the FWAZM PLAGR MNTLU text of the message into something that looked like real navy speak. This was by no means the first such message Admiral Townsend had received, but it was the first time he'd actually had his communications officer bring him the code book so he could decrypt it himself.

The Chief of Staff brought the chart to the admiral's stateroom along with the operations officer, there was no need to involve anyone else at this stage of the game. The admiral marked the spot on the chart that *Montpelier* had suggested in the message and saw that it was a day's transit west of the battle group's current position. According to John Cushman, that spot was deep enough for good acoustics even in the warm waters of the Mediterranean, and that would allow his ASW destroyers, his ASW helos and his S3 ASW jets to prosecute the Soviet sub, augmented by the "Woodpeckers" from VP 49 flying from Sigonella. They'd be the perfect trap, now all he had to do was coax that damned AGI over to this part of the Balearic Basin so it could watch the show ... and play "tattletale" in the little play that Cushman had concocted. Well, the AGI seemed to be obsessed with *Ike* anyway; wherever she went, the dingy little spy ship seemed to follow along like a droopy hound dog. He'd have to play the last few hours craftily though, so that *Ike* would draw the Soviet scow to the right spot.

CHAPTER 16
READY FOR TURNOVER

"REMEMBER MARTY WE'LL ONLY HAVE time for a tiny bit of normal daily ship's business when we get to Rota and begin turnover. There must be thousands of pages we'll need to handle, plus I have a safe filled with classified messages that I'm custodian for. The captain only keeps a very few documents in his safe. We've got the bulk of everything he needs, the operations department has a ton more of stuff than we do, but we have what the captain needs as ready reference. We'll have to page check every one of the Med Pubs that we're handing over to *Indy* but let me tell you that when I relieved as captain's yeoman the shipment of Med Pubs was in a huge cardboard box sitting right here on the table. The ARFCOS guy just dumped it and when I opened it I found that none of the changes had been entered in the pubs going back almost four years, what a pain!

It took me a day and a half, just to get that squared away. Then I made an index of all the pubs and I had the ops officer send a message to ComSixthFlt verifying that the changes I put in, brought them all up to date. I stapled a copy of the answering message to the index, so that's our proof that the pubs are all current. We have to turn all that over to the *Indy* guy and the captain is counting on us to make that turnover smooth and error free."

"I know Sam but with the two of us it should go pretty quickly."

Wilson shook her head, "It can only go as fast as the yeoman on

Indy lets us go, remember he or she will have to double check everything we give them. Hopefully we'll get someone who knows how to do the checks and isn't some lazy-ass politician who sits there and makes us do all the work or even worse just sits there on his ass and slows us down with a bunch of BS about how great he is and how much he knows."

"I know what you mean Sam, but I'm sure you can swing enough weight to head off anything like that. I've seen how you are able to keep even the most officious twerps in the ship's office minding their own business and when that lieutenant from the training department came in that time screaming bloody murder about lost records, you backed him down and then he apologized for everything because you showed him exactly why he was wrong."

Wilson giggled, "Yeah that was pretty sweet but it wouldn't have worked out that way if I had messed up even a semicolon on those papers he was so sure he never got." She thought for a second, "You know Marty that's really the secret of making it work right in the navy. You know what to do, you do your best, and you do the honorable thing; you don't try to back door stuff and you take responsibility for your own actions."

Fernandez meant it, "Thank you Sam for everything you've taught me and everything you've done for me. Without you I probably would have ended up as just a compartment cleaner for the admin department or some asterisk on the watch bill in the ship's office."

Wilson smiled, it was nice to have one of her contemporaries say thank you for something she had done. She did favors for people all the time, and she never expected thanks in return, but it seemed to her that simple politeness made every day better. Thinking back over her service onboard it was the thing that she loved most; well not quite most, but right up there with finding her love and being recognized for her swimming heroics and … no what she loved most was being part of the crew and doing what the captain needed her to do and what her shipmates needed her to do.

"Marty thank you for saying that, but the truth is that you're a great worker and you're a great shipmate. I'm glad you're my relief. I wouldn't dream of leaving the captain in lesser hands."

They only had one last big project to finish before they would be ready to conduct turnover and it had nothing to do with the *Indy* inchoppers. The captain had marked up a copy of his "Standing Orders to the Officer of the Deck" and it would take a day to make the changes. It was a document that had been produced on manual typewriters and had never been stored to magnetic cards. They'd have to type it from scratch. Wilson decided she wanted to do the job herself, she'd be able to learn something as she knocked out the pages.

The captain had been on the bridge almost round the clock for the last three days and the level of flight ops activity had been higher than Wilson could remember since they'd entered the Med. It was even more intense than during the Sinkex they'd participated in before their port visit to Mallorca. All their squadrons were playing in it too, even the S3s and she knew that they were the ASW jets. Hardly a half-hour went by without a slew of launches and landings.

The talk on the mess decks was that this frenetic pace wasn't a planned exercise either, normally when there was to be a NATO or unilateral exercise there was information floating around in advance pointing to it. This time there was no mention of anything like that, not even during the department head meetings. Wilson had a feeling something was up but she had no hints from anyone what it might be. She'd even intercepted the captain's mess supervisor and carried a mug of soup and a sandwich to the boss up on the bridge, but he didn't offer to shed any light on the mystery.

She'd even had to postpone their rehearsals during the last few hectic days. Her cast was too bushed after their watches to be much good on stage. Stef Turner was standing watch and watch with all the other plane handlers and when she joined Wilson and their friends on the mess decks she had almost fallen asleep in her supper. Wilson wondered how long they could keep it up. Surely things would break, hopefully no one would get hurt in some big accident.

She was on the bridge showing the captain the revised standing orders when helos from their ASW squadron took off, headed for a submarine prosecution zone just over the horizon.

Captain Christensen handed her his binoculars, "Look right over there Sam, it's an old friend come by to test us I suppose."

She pointed the glasses and steadied them in the direction the captain had indicated. She recognized the small gray ship right away. It was the same stupid AGI that had dogged their operations since they'd come to the Med. She wondered where the little scow went when the battle group took a break for a port visit. "Captain where does the AGI go when we head into port?"

He looked at her and grinned, "I don't think it goes very far, their whole reason for being is to keep track of us and blow the whistle when the balloon goes up so that a sub, or plane or surface ship can take us out with a short range nuke. Our job is to survive that if it happens, and we will. He, on the other hand, is going to go out in a geyser of flame and seawater as soon as that balloon goes up and he knows it."

She thought the captain's description of their differing roles was chilling, certainly the sailors on that Russian spy ship were expected to do their duty just as she and her shipmates were. "Captain I wouldn't want to have their job to save my life. At least we have the ability to say we are part of the fight, part of the attack force; all they can claim is that they are sneaky little spies. I'd hate that, there's no honor in that at all."

"I know Sam, but remember the *Pueblo* and the *Liberty*, both were US intelligence gathering ships and they did their duty too. *Pueblo's* people were locked up in North Korea for years and *Liberty* lost 34 crew killed. Those men had no chance by themselves and not one finger was lifted by anyone in the chain of command to help them." He clenched his jaw after he said it.

Wilson had forgotten both incidents, "I understand Captain, and if ever I get to have a responsible place in the navy and something like that happens to one of my ships, I'm ordering the cavalry in with guns a blazin' and right bloody now!"

Just then the phone by the captain's chair buzzed and he picked it up. It was the flag watch officer ordering Ike to set EMCON condition Alfa as soon as the last of their aircraft were recovered from their sorties against Sardinia. Christensen passed the order on to the OOD. It was enough to cause the captain to wonder what was going on, the AGI certainly knew where they were so it had nothing to do with him. Moments later the flag ordered the rest of the battle group to set EMCON Alfa as well. Christensen knew something serious was going on then. EMCON condition Alfa shut down all electronic emissions from the battle group. Only their helos would still be out there squawking and using their radars.

Wilson heard the exchange, "What does it mean for us Captain?"

He wasn't sure but he knew she was as curious as he was, "Sam I think it means that the admiral is doing something crafty."

"SONAR CONN, PREPARE TO GO active on Master One."

"Conn sonar aye, powering up the BQQ-5 active."

Commander Cushman was impatient to close his side of the trap on the bumbling boob they had dogged all the way from the northern climes of the Atlantic. There had been no change in his daily routine and his BOZO factor had not improved at all. The running joke on the mess decks was that the poor schmucks had gotten a bad lot of vodka and it had effected their brains, after all that must have been what had happened to Lupo, only he'd fried his on torpedo alcohol.

"Conn sonar, ready to hammer Master One, tri-beam Omni!"

"Sonar conn aye, bang 'em."

The bing, bang, bong, BOWWANGG made the lights dim slightly and was followed by another loud sequence as the Q5 active operator punched their nemesis a second time. Everyone aboard heard the distinctive sound and anybody within miles that had a sonar turned on and listening yanked off his headset and started rubbing his ears.

"Conn sonar, Master One bears zero eight niner, range one niner hundred yards."

The XO nodded as the PK operator dialed in the spot to their range solution, they'd had it within a hundred yards, even without the pinging.

"Sonar conn, aye. Secure pinging, keep the five in standby."

"Secure pinging, remain in standby, conn sonar aye."

Cushman looked at the PPI scope and nodded his head, "Nav it looks like the admiral's got an active buoy field in over here." He dragged the tip of his grease pencil down the line of points to the north, "And here are his choppers banging away and leapfrogging in on the turkey."

He "Xd" the three hi-frequency indications on the display where the choppers were dipping their active pingers and made his decision.

"Nav let's get up to comms depth and let the admiral know we think it's time for the pièce de résistance."

The navigator took the ship up into the seastate and the slow easy roll was apparent as they got to sixty two feet and raised the UHF mast. It only took a moment and their transmission was gone and dumping out on the teletype in Ike's flag communications space. The communications watch officer rogered for the message and immediately called flag plot on the 24MC.

"Admiral, *Montpelier* reports all is in readiness for phase two."

Admiral Townsend smiled and acknowledged the report, turning to the flag watch officer. "Recall the helos and tell the S3s to secure their buoys. Get everybody on deck and then it's a hard EMCON Alfa, execute the get outta town portion of the plan."

An hour later the only ships still left in the area were a bewildered AGI and a badly shaken Bozo. The battle group had already hauled off over the horizon and *Montpelier* conducted a hot turnover to a P3C from VP 49 who would follow the hapless sub all the way to the Gulf of Sidra.

Wilson left the bridge when the captain did. All their helos and the S3s were aboard and Ike was making almost forty knots headed west, they would clear the area quickly and then the admiral would regather the battle group. "Well Captain I hope you can get some rest tonight, you look a little worn out."

He chuckled, "I'm fine Sam and I will grab some bunk time, but first I have to go put in an appearance on the mess decks. Tonight is pizza night and I'm serving the troops."

She knew he liked to interact with the crew like that whenever he could, "Captain I'll come help and I'll get Marty to come and serve too. Then we'll take over and you can walk around in the mess for a bit before you go get some rest. Don't worry I'll make sure everyone knows you made all the pizzas yourself."

Christensen laughed, "You don't have to tell them that Sam, besides I only made the pepperoni ones."

On the mess decks there was a mood of buoyancy and excitement, it was almost the feeling that abides in a locker room when the team wins it's hardest season game and realizes it just made the playoffs. Everything wasn't over just yet, they still had a few days before they would rendezvous with the relieving battle group but the crew could tell they were in the home stretch. The hard part of their deployment was behind them.

Even the most grizzled salts were anxious to be on their way home. They hadn't lost a plane or a pilot and no one had been hurt. The only close run thing this whole deployment had been losing Sam Wilson and her other "Sixth Fleet Seven" pals back in the Bay of Naples but she'd gotten them all back to the battle group and the proof of that was seeing her laughing and joking with all the sailors in the chow line, as she stood between that new yeoman and the captain, serving up slices of pizza to them. By this time, of course, everybody knew her. She'd gotten those awards a month ago and many of them had seen her down in the gym duking it out with Bates or playing basketball, and if that wasn't enough, you could see her with the cast of that comic opera everybody was talking about. Many of them who hadn't been lucky enough to see even the early rehearsals were anxious to because they had heard that many of their shipmates were in the cast. Hell the admiral himself was playing the big cheese in the show!

The captain stayed with Wilson and Fernandez dishing out the pizza until the off going watch was fed. Pizza night was always popular and the supply department tried to schedule at least one or two every month. Wilson knew from her look at the ship's roster that they had crew members from every ethnic group there is, but everyone seemed to love the pizza. Some of their cooks had even tried to make it the way they had learned watching the greatest pizza chefs in the world during *Ike's* visit to Naples.

Master Chief Connolly walked over to the serving line to share a thought with the captain, "This is a great way to end our Med operations Captain, some good food and some good spirits. I think morale is as high as I've ever seen it."

Christensen smiled, "I agree Master Chief, now we just have to conduct a smart turnover and have a safe run home." He looked at Wilson then, "And we have to put on the show for everyone. By the way Sam, Admiral Wilkins and Admiral Morton will be aboard for turnover and they'll both want to see the show."

Wilson almost gulped, how could the captain hold out the knowledge that the fleet commander and the commander of all naval forces in Europe would be front and center for her show? Talk about *pressure!*

She smiled and shrugged, "Well maybe that's a good thing, after all, Admiral Wilkins is my favorite 'three star' and I'll get to meet Admiral Morton, maybe I can make him my favorite 'four star'."

She turned to the captain, "Captain why don't you go and get some rest, Marty and the Master Chief can handle everything and if they have a problem I'll be here to help them."

The captain left laughing and headed for his stateroom, he knew everything was in safe hands.

★ ★ ★ ★

"CONN, RADIO ALL TRAFFIC'S ON board, ready to go deep."

The OOD could see that the UHF mast was sliding into its housing in the sail and he lowered the 'scope. "Diving Officer, make your depth six seven zero feet. Helm all ahead full. Left fifteen degrees rudder steady course zero eight five."

The 21MC bleated again, "Conn radio, Captain to radio."

Warner unlocked the door and the captain slipped in and went immediately to the teletype. "Another COWCATCHER Warner?"

"Yes Sir just flip it on and it'll print out. Want me to leave Captain?"

"No Warner just give me a second and if I'm right I'll have an outgoing for you to cut."

The teletype clacked out the short message and he flipped it off and tore the sheet from the continuous roll of yellow paper. "It's broadcast number six eighty one for your log Petty Officer Warner, come to the wardroom in twenty minutes and we'll have that outgoing for you."

"Aye, aye Captain."

Warner thought it was funny, he'd had the watch when every one of those COWCATCHER messages had come in and that probably meant that someone at the BCA, also standing six hour watches, had sent every one of them. Weird.

Commander Cushman looked at the chart in the control room and made his decision. The message released Montpelier from the mission. Apparently Bozo had been so spooked by the reception he'd received in the Med he'd had to contact his boss and find out what to do, and then he'd taken off at maximum speed to run home to momma. VP 49 would track him all the way to the sub tender.

Warner cut the message that reported they were proceeding to Rota to return to the battle group and they sent it immediately. If they ran fast and deep they could catch up with *Ike* and they could enter the Gulf of Cadiz together, just like old times.

The afternoon before they were due to enter the Gulf and anchor off Rota Spain, Wilson had the cast run through their final dress rehearsal. Everything went off like clockwork and the portion of the crew that had been invited to see the show during the afternoon watch cheered and applauded their efforts. The funny bits had been hilarious and the voices of the cast had been as good as any light opera company could have been. Wilson couldn't have been prouder of them all.

CHAPTER 17
FRIENDS IN NEED

IT WAS ALMOST WALL TO wall admirals in Ike's flag spaces as Commander Cushman described the handover of the Type IV Soviet nuke to the P3C and thanked Admiral Townsend for setting the trap that *Montpelier* had chased the poor dumb cluck into when they'd blasted the ocean with their active sonar pings.

"Admiral it was like I had just told my sonarman he'd won the anchor pool. The adrenalin he'd stored up was almost palpable and then after he banged him and he skedaddled, it was like the fourth of July."

Admiral Townsend smiled as his submarine skipper flipped to the next slide in his briefing package. They'd agreed to keep it at the Genser level, the COWCATCHER data had been sanitized and packaged as soon as they'd tied up in Rota. The box of tapes and logged data had been spirited off by the armed courier and placed in a padlocked steel box before he lugged it onto a plane that was headed to an ultra-secret facility in Maryland. There a battalion of analysts would fold, spindle and mutilate the data, trying to make sense of the different acoustic jabberwocky.

Cushman's next slide was a listing of the really dumb things that they had detected Bozo doing during the days that *Montpelier* had been in contact with him. "Here's the list Admiral and the things we've identified are in decreasing order of stupidity, at least from a submariner's point of view."

---

1. Unable to control depth—systems problem?
2. Standard security search doctrine disregarded.
3. No understanding of sound properties in water.
4. Personal conduct appalling.

Admiral Wilkins latched on to the first item, "What do you make of that John? Could it be that the design of their ship control system is inadequate or is it just that their sailors aren't trained to operate it?"

"Admiral that's exactly why I put the question mark there. I had no way to determine which it is or if it's a combination of both. Hopefully the analysts will be able to figure it out. It was really scary watching them go up to periscope depth in any kind of sea state at all. They'd fly and then they'd plunge like a rock and it happened every time. It was almost as if nobody onboard was ever introduced to the concept of compensating for the changes in buoyancy as a submarine changes depth. That's submariner 101 and I think they all flunked it."

Admiral Townsend grinned as his skipper explained his first item, he remembered how the planesmen, the diving officer, the chief of the watch and the OOD had worked together so closely to get Montpelier to periscope depth in order to do the things that had to be done to transfer him back to his flagship with the two women sailors he now thought of almost as daughters. "John what do you really think it is, design or training?"

Cushman shrugged, "Jesus Admiral I sure *hope* it's in the design, to think that it's something they could fix by just getting rid of a bunch of incompetents or by instigating a decent training regimen would be discouraging."

Admiral Morton had flown down from London to attend the briefing too and he was clearly pleased with *Montpelier's* recent success against the highly vaunted Soviet sub. "What about the security doctrine item Captain?"

Cushman grinned, "Admiral the guy didn't clear his baffles even once while we were watching him. Now I can understand being careless, and I could even buy in to stupid and inexperienced, but not to have done it even *routinely* a couple times a watch says to me criminally negligent. Even the worst-run ship keeps a watch all around."

Admiral Hatch had flown over from Naples and his CTF 69 headquarters where he ran the show for all the submarines in the Mediterranean when they weren't attached to the battle groups. He was very interested in understanding the Soviet sub, "What about the noise John?"

"Abysmal Admiral, he shot his TDU after every meal and the sound was like a dump truck unloading a load of nuts and bolts. No one aboard understood how to make the tin cans and other junk he jettisoned keep from making noise; light bulbs popping, the whole works. Just plain abysmal. And as to that last item, hey I just ran into a sailor who was underway with us for only two days and she knew better submariner noise habits in that short time than any of the clowns on Bozo."

Admiral Townsend smiled, he could only be talking about Sam Wilson. He knew that Commander Cushman had just had lunch with Captain Christensen in *Ike's* captain's mess before the briefing and he was sure Admiral Wilkins would remember she had ridden *Montpelier* with him but Admiral Morton might not recall. "Admiral he's talking about Yeoman Third Sam Wilson who went with me to visit Prime Minister Begin when *Montpelier* was in Ashdod in June. She and Personnelman Second Dorothy Stanfield both rode for two days before we rejoined the battlegroup and we transferred to *Ike*. They're the first two women to serve on a submarine and I was honored to be a part of it."

Admiral Morton chuckled, "I remember Tommy, and I remember thinking we'd never hear the last of it from the pencil pushers in DC, but it played really big because it was connected to that great press that Stanfield and what was that other sailor's name, 'Manka something'? earned by their heroics in Israel."

Admiral Townsend and Commander Cushman answered at the same time, "Manckowicz Admiral, Ted Manckowicz."

Cushman elaborated, "He's the strongest sailor in the fleet and probably the luckiest too Admiral. He's marrying that little personnelman when we get back to the states, quite the dish."

Admiral Townsend chuckled and nodded in agreement. "Both those girls are quite something to look at but the quality starts *inside* in each of them."

Cushman smiled, "Yes Sir, I just stopped by Chris's mess to thank Sam Wilson earlier, for saving *Montpelier* from a fate worse than death. Somehow one of the reels of that movie we shared with the embassy folks in Algiers got misplaced and she got it back for us. My COB wants to adopt her and all my single guys want to marry her, especially the guy that she got out of hot water."

Admiral Townsend was shaking his head, "That woman is right at the center of everything good that's happened in this battle group our whole time here. She even helped put out that fire on *Ike's* weather deck in Algiers. I just endorsed Chris Christensen's recommendation for a Meritorious Service Medal for her, it's probably in your in basket Admiral."

Admiral Wilkins was nodding, "Yes! I just forwarded it before I flew to Rota. It's probably in the mail to London right now."

Admiral Morton hadn't seen it yet but he was surely interested, "She must be an exceptional sailor if she's got all you guys singing her praises. I'd like to meet her too."

Admiral Townsend smiled, "She'll be at the show tonight Admiral, I hope you're staying around long enough to watch it. Tonight's performance is for the rest of *Ike's* crew who haven't seen the rehearsal and the folks in the battle group who care to attend. Tomorrow's show is for the people from *Indy* and her escorts."

The four star chuckled, "Tommy when I heard about the show I had them make my travel arrangements. I wouldn't miss seeing you in a classic like *Pinafore,* for all the tea in China!"

Wilson was just finishing the last of the show programs when the knock on the office door caused her to look up as it was opened, "Excuse me are you too busy to see me Miss Wilson?"

She recognized him immediately, "Goodness no Sir, come right in! How are you Mr. Nagle?"

"I'm fine thank you Miss, I've come to thank you for what you did for me back in Algiers. I really didn't understand that whole thing about the movie reel, but the captain told me what a mess it would have been if it really did get lost and didn't make it back to *Montpelier.* I had no idea that it was such a big deal!"

Wilson had no real experience in psychology but she could tell from her previous day's involvement with Nagle that he was unsure of himself, he just wasn't very experienced with people. She hoped he would be able to overcome that soon, his sailors deserved a leader with some confidence in himself. She gave him her best it's-no-big-deal smile, "Please sit down Sir, would you like some coffee?"

"Oh, no I don't want to be any trouble. I just came over to *Ike* to get some things at your ship's store."

She was about to say it wasn't any trouble at all when the door opened and Chief Owens, her virtuoso Captain Cochrane, came in. "Sam we're all set for tonight, I just ran the Tars through the opening dance number in costume and they were better than ever, you know counting our four new volunteers there are twenty of 'em now; thank goodness you had those extra costumes made last month!"

He was in his blue, epauletted costume with it's white knee-length breeches, and he looked like he'd just stepped out of the 19th Century. Wilson thought he looked the image of the perfect *right good Captain.* "Oh Chief that's wonderful! You know I was a little skeptical when we first started out recruiting our cast. I thought the guys might think the Tars were silly but your choreography made it popular. We had guys sign up when they saw you running the dancing rehearsals. Besides being my favorite Chief Machinist you are my *second* favorite Captain."

Nagle wasn't quite sure what was going on but he'd heard of the show that was being put on later that evening and he was planning to attend with a bunch of other *Porter* officers. Wilson made introductions, "Mr. Nagle this is Chief Owens he's in the show and you'll see him tonight if you come. Chief this is Ensign Nagle from *Porter*. He helped me recover from a bad situation back in Algiers."

The Chief held out his hand, "Nice to meet you Sir, are you coming to the show tonight?"

"Hello Chief it's good to meet you too. I was planning on coming over later with some of the other *Porter* officers. I'm here now because I came to go to your ship's store. I wanted to come and see Miss Wilson to thank her for getting me out of serious trouble."

Wilson laughed, "Oh Sir, I told you it was *you* who helped *me* and I really appreciated that and I've told you at least ten times, *please* call me Sam!"

She turned to the smiling chief, "Don't we know someone who is handling the tickets tonight Chief? Maybe we can get Mr. Nagle a seat in our 'dress circle' what do you think?"

He chuckled, "Sam I think if you wanted anything to happen in this whole battle group, all it would take is a word from you in the right place. I'll tell the Master Chief you want Mr. Nagle to have a place right in the VIP section."

"Excellent, it's settled then! Mr. Nagle come to the hangar deck at 1830 and just ask for Master Chief Connolly. He'll see that you get the best seat in the house!"

Chief Owens finished it up for her, "Yes Sir, and just say that Sam said so!"

The chief took his leave and Wilson had a million other things to see to. "Mr. Nagle I have some things to do Sir, I'm waiting for some helpers to carry a couple of boxes of programs for me and then

I have to lock up and go do other things. I'll see you later Sir, by the way, what's your first name?"

Nagle was surprised by the question but he saw no harm in answering it, "It's Michael, Sam. Thank you for the chat and I'll ask for the master chief tonight, but now I'd better go find your ship's store."

Fernandez opened the door then and was followed in by three sailors from the deck division, they had come to carry the boxes of programs to the hangar deck.

Wilson motioned to the boxes, "Guys you know to take these to the hangar deck right?"

The first class bo'sun's mate nodded, "Yes Sam we'll make sure they're safe and out of the way, the master chief showed us where."

She smiled, "Thank you Bob, that's one more thing to check off. Oh let me have a few of those before you go, please, I'll run them up to the flag spaces for our visitors."

She grabbed a few of the programs as they left headed for the companionway and the hangar deck. Wilson turned back to Nagle, "Sir this is Marty Fernandez, she's my assistant for the next few weeks until I'm transferred, if you'd like she could show you the way to our ship's store."

Fernandez nodded grinning, "Sure Mr. Nagle follow me I need to pick up a few things there myself."

When Wilson got to the flag spaces Commander Cushman had just finished answering the last of the admirals' questions and the chief of staff motioned to a lieutenant to open the briefing room door. Now that the briefing was completed they could all get back to turnover. It was a good thing they were here in Rota, with the number of admirals who had come to attend the briefing they were hard pressed to find enough staterooms to house them all. The Rota naval air station BOQ's VIP quarters helped ease that problem and there were several good hotels within a few minutes of the base. It was one less problem for the chief of staff to worry about.

Wilson saw him coming out of the briefing room, "Hello Captain Mallory, I have some programs for the show tonight I thought I would bring them up and give them to you so you can pass them to the admiral and his guests."

The chief of staff was about to take them when Admiral Townsend emerged with Commander Cushman, they were both smiling. Cushman went first, "Sam! It's great to see you! Thank you again for getting us that reel back, you have to know that you pulled our fat out of the fire doing that. Every man on board owes you a debt of gratitude and the COB wants to adopt you! Can you come and have dinner with us one evening at least before we get underway for the states? We'd all like to repay your kindness."

Admiral Townsend cut in then, "John you can't have her tonight or tomorrow night, she's putting on our show. Bring your guys over, it's going to be even better than when we did it in Algiers!"

The other admirals joined them then, Admiral Wilkin's face brightened immediately, "Sam! How are you, they tell me you've been quite busy since you saved our bacon for us back in Naples!"

She laughed her gay laugh as she took his hand, "Goodness Admiral it's great to see you again! How did your shopping go in Palma? I hope you're coming to see the show tonight, I've brought some show programs for you."

Admiral Morton cut in then, "So you're the Sam Wilson everybody's been telling me about. Rumor is you're involved in the production tonight. Admiral Townsend says you're an absolute slave driver!"

She laughed with him as he shook her hand warmly, "Believe me this is a happy day for all of us and Commander Cushman says you helped the morale on his ship like nobody ever has."

She'd never met him before but she knew who he was of course, she'd read the bio sheet on him that she kept in the captain's briefing book. "Admiral Morton it's wonderful to finally meet you but I think any notoriety I may have gotten is way out of proportion to what I really deserve. I'm just happy to be a good shipmate Sir."

The only person in the little band of senior sailors surrounding her who believed what she'd just said was Wilson herself.

Admiral Wilkins wondered, "Sam can I have one of those programs please? I'm guessing they'll be worth their weight in gold after the show is history."

She handed him one and passed one to each of the other admirals and the chief of staff. She had one left as they all started looking them over. "We're the Task Group Sixty Point Two Light Opera Company gentlemen, and I would be honored if you would each autograph my copy of the program."

That night she could see them all right up front, as the crowd waited expectantly for Master Chief Connolly's introduction and the opening overture; there were Dorothy and Ted and there was Ensign Nagle too, right between the fleet commander and the submarine group admiral. She hoped he would enjoy the show and perhaps the other thing she had planned would help his self-esteem.

After the master chief made his introduction she stepped to the middle of the stage and looked out at the sea of faces, her shipmates and men and women from all the other ships in the task group, and made her sweeping bow to them all, "Shipmates, esteemed guests and all of you who have helped in the production of this show; we are the Task Group Sixty Point Two Light Opera Company and we welcome you to tonight's production of *HMS Pinafore*. Some of you may know it as *'The lass who loved a sailor'*. We'll take a short intermission after the first act and Master Chief Connolly has arranged some beverage distribution then as well, but don't go far from your places because we'll be ready to get into the second act *right soon!* Now one last thing, we dedicate this performance to all our good shipmates and especially to Ensign Michael Nagle, of the *Porter*, the newest officer in the battle group and a great friend and shipmate."

She turned to her orchestra leader, bowed and pointed her plumed hat at her, "Maestro it's all yours."

The opening strains poured forth, amplified by the extra speakers that the IC-men had hurried to put in under the tall ceiling of the hangar deck. Chief Owen's Tars wielded their choreographed swabs and the audience was caught up in it all by the time they finished their salty: *"WE SAIL THE OCEAN BLUE AND OUR SAUCY SHIP'S A BEAUTY!"* Chief Owen's *"MY GALLANT CREW GOOD MORNING"* greeting and the ensuing repartee was well received and the Admiral's entrance as Sir Joseph with his retinue of adoring distaff relatives was hilarious. Bate's prolonged piping with the comic breath in the middle had the admirals clutching their sides and Wilson could see almost all the audience trying to sing along during Sir Joseph's *"WHEN I WAS A LAD..."* . When he got to the last verse and it's advice for young men to: *"STAY CLOSE TO YOUR DESKS AND NEVER GO TO SEA ... AND YOU CAN BE THE RULER OF THE QUEEN'S NAVEE!"* ... he had the whole hangar deck laughing and applauding. Everyone seemed in love with her Josephine, and Chief Sutton's Little Buttercup character had the whole audience cracking up. Wilson couldn't have been prouder of them. But the best part of it all was that whenever she looked at Captain Christensen he was laughing and if she could make him enjoy the show, it had all been worthwhile.

During the intermission she stepped down from the stage and shook hands with her admiral guests and picked up on a scrap of conversation between Admiral Morton and Admiral Wilkins. It seemed that Admiral Wilkins was retiring at the end of the year and it would leave his job as ComSixthFlt open. Wilson knew that it would take a nomination for the Fleet Commander's job and action by the US Senate to promote a Rear Admiral to three star rank to fill it. She wondered who would be nominated, surely it would take someone special, someone who was not only a great leader but also someone who knew his bluejackets and would keep their welfare and the readiness of the navy first and foremost in his mind. She didn't know who the navy might nominate, but she certainly knew who *she* would.

CHAPTER 18
WHAT ELSE IS A SENATOR FOR?

WILSON THANKED THEM ALL FOR coming when she took her bow with the master chief after her cast had taken their last curtain call. The greater part of the audience was streaming down the companionway headed for the mess decks and those who had arrived from other ships in the battle group headed for the boom where they would catch a liberty launch or their own ship's boats back to their commands. A helo would take the admirals ashore who were billeted there overnight. She thanked Admiral Townsend for his inspired performance and he walked out into the remaining men and women in the audience in his ornate gold-bedecked costume, shaking hands with many of them on his way to the flag spaces.

She held up her hand and signaled the rest of the cast to gather around her for an important conversation, "Everybody you were great tonight and I know you've got other things to do but I need you to do something for me before the curtain tomorrow night. I need you to write down your name and address back home and the names of your Senators. I have all the *Ike* crew names and addresses, but I need the ones from you others that aren't *Ike* crewmembers and I need your Senators' names and addresses if you can find them. I'll explain later but we are about to start a letter campaign with the Senate to help the navy."

She spent the next few hours drafting the individual letters that her cast members would send in an attempt to place a name they all knew in the forefront as their next fleet commander. She began by drafting her own:

---

9 November 1983
Aboard *USS Eisenhower*
Anchored off Rota, Spain

Dear Mrs. Gressley,

I am the Captain's Yeoman on *Ike* and I'm writing to you because I would like you to intercede with the Senator on an item of critical importance to the navy and to our country. I understand it is highly irregular to write to you but I am realistic enough to know that most offices don't run with the precision and speed that mine does. I know that the quickest way to place an idea before the Senator is through you.

I am writing to seek the Senator's help in choosing the next Commander of the Sixth Fleet. I know that billet will be open by the end of the year because the current Commander, Vice Admiral Wilkins, is retiring from the navy. I am writing to suggest that Rear Admiral Thomas Townsend be advanced to Vice Admiral and named to that post.

Admiral Townsend is not only an outstanding leader and model sailor, he is the perfect choice to be the top sailor in the Mediterranean because he has a total grasp of the problems and peculiarities in that part of the world. He has a way of carrying himself that inspires others and he recently achieved a special relationship with the Prime Minister of Israel and has become friends with the Governor General of Mallorca and the Prime Minister of Algeria as well.

I have a personal reason for my recommendation too. I am a woman sailor and Admiral Townsend is *the most pro*-women-sailors officer in the navy. Several months ago I was marooned with another woman sailor and five men (the newspapers called us the "Sixth Fleet Seven"). We were lost for four days and Admiral Townsend not only insisted on finding us and bringing us safely back, he called the parents of each of us and made sure they understood all he was doing to find us. He puts the safety and welfare of his bluejackets above everything else.

My parents live in Corning Iowa and you can call my mother if you'd like, she will tell you how the admiral's thoughtfulness helped her when she was frantic with worry.

Thank you ma'am for your kind attention to this matter I hope you will help me and every other sailor in the Sixth Fleet by telling your husband about this outstanding and deserving Naval Officer and encouraging the Senator to use his connections with the navy to push for his nomination; and then by voting for his appointment.

Sincerely yours,

Samantha Wilson YN3 USN

PS I will be coming home on leave for Thanksgiving and I would enjoy speaking to you about this matter by phone or in person at your home, if you'd like.
SAW

Wilson printed out the letter and then another very much like it for Mrs. Jepson, she only changed a few phrases so that if the two Iowa Senators' wives compared notes, they would see she hadn't just copied them. Then she built the boiler plate for each of the letters to the Senators in the other forty nine states. She just had to find a sailor from Idaho and one from New Mexico to sign the ones to those Senators' wives.

The bulk of the next morning was busy with the business of

turnover. Wilson let Fernandez deal directly with YN1 Collins, the captain's yeoman from *Independence,* reviewing each of the publications to be turned over. It took a few hours to prove to him that each of the publications was up to snuff. Afterward both Wilson and Fernandez helped carry the boxes of publications and documents to the quarterdeck. There they found that Collins would have to wait until the next boat from *Indy* arrived in order to ferry him back with the boxes. *Indy's* boats weren't running on a regular schedule so the wait might be a long one.

Wilson checked with the OOD, "Excuse me Sir what boats are alongside now at the boom? I'm trying to arrange a ride for Petty Officer Collins and his classified material back to *Indy*."

The officer knew exactly, "Sam the captain's gig, the barge and the relieving admiral's barge are alongside. Also there are two of our fifty footers, one is getting underway for Rota in five minutes."

"Thank you Mr. Castro, may I use your phone?"

"Sure thing Sam, it's right over there." He gestured to a watchstander who assisted her with her call and five minutes later, Bates and Holden arrived and helped carry the boxes down the ladder to the boom. The gig was underway immediately and it took ten minutes to make the trip to *Indy*. Collins was so impressed that he didn't even ask them to help him carry the boxes up the ladder to *Indy's* quarterdeck.

"Hey thanks you guys you sure made that easy, your captain must be a pretty neat guy to let you use his gig any time you want."

Wilson was quick, "Marty is a special part of the captain's staff Petty Officer Collins and she has his ear on all things administrative. Don't forget to come and see the show tonight. The crowd last night loved it and I think Admiral Lane is going to be here to see it. I know your captain will be, he's meeting with our captain right now."

The senior petty officer knew he should have known that and was crestfallen, "Thanks for the invite Wilson, I'll come over after chow."

"I think you'll have fun Petty Officer Collins, my friend Petty

Officer Bates here is one of the stars." Then she drew him aside and put her mouth to his ear.

She spoke softly and very calmly to him "*Ike* is coming back to the Med next year and if she relieves *Indy* I want you to make sure that the pubs are in as good a shape as when you got them. Marta will have the responsibility for it all then and she'll probably have a new captain by that time too. I'd consider it a personal favor if you would do everything you can to have those pubs squared away for her."

Collins nodded, "I understand Wilson I'll do my best."

"Thank you, I'll take you at your word. Have fun at our show tonight and have a great navy day."

Fernandez sat next to Wilson on the trip back to *Ike*.

"Sam what did you say to him?"

"Nothing Marty, just that he'd better do his job right because if he messes up even one of those pubs you'll catch it and make him look foolish." She laughed then, "Don't worry Marty you're ten times smarter than he is, you'll find whatever he fouls up easily and then if he gives you any crap you just go get Chief Thomas and if that doesn't work your new captain will back you to the hilt. Captain Christensen trusts you implicitly and so will your new boss."

"Thanks Sam, listen I know I owe you everything for teaching me how to do this job and I will forever be grateful to you. I'm gonna miss you after you leave. Thank you for having faith in me."

Wilson gave her a hug, "You did it Marty, all on your own. You're getting that medal too for helping during the fire. It was great knowing you were right there with me up on *Monty's* sail."

Bates idled in to the boom then and Terri Holden jumped out to make them fast. Wilson and Fernandez climbed out and headed up the accommodation ladder. There was still plenty to do for the rest of the day. Fernandez paused after saluting the OOD, "Sam I'll handle the rest of the mail now and afterward I want to scrub and wax the deck in the office, if you want to go gather your letter writers I'll be fine."

Bates came up behind them, "What do you need from me Sam?"

"Billy if you can come with me I'll give you what I worked up for your letters to your Senators, you can look them over and add your own thoughts and I'll make the changes, then you can sign them and we'll mail all of them together before we get underway to head home."

She knew that Rota was the hub for all military flights coming in to the Med from the states and everything headed back staged through Rota too. Her Senate mail campaign would be well underway before they left for Norfolk. By the end of the afternoon she had the rough drafts for over half the letters they would send. It would only take an hour or so for her to smooth them up and have them ready for her fellow conspirators in the morning. They wouldn't be getting underway until after noon chow so she would have plenty of time to finish the envelopes and get the stack to the postal clerks. She felt a tingling in her spine when she thought about it, her favorite admiral would be getting an early promotion and he would be going to a job he would excel in. If everything worked right, it would happen before Congress left on their Christmas break. She thought of it as her present to the sailors of the Sixth Fleet.

The boats bringing sailors from the *Indy* and her escort ships began arriving just before the end of evening chow. Wilson ate only lightly, she was anxious to gather her cast and get set for the final performance of their show. This would be their "Gold" show, put on to entertain their reliefs. Rear Admiral Lane, his staff and some of the officers from his air squadrons would be there too. She hoped that the inchoppers would enjoy the show as much as her shipmates and the others in her own battlegroup had. Hey if they only liked it half as much she would feel they had done well. She had a pride of ownership in their production, she thought her feelings were the same as one of the Broadway or Hollywood directors might be for their big expensive productions. Hers had cost next to nothing and the rehearsals, and all the work to put it on by everyone involved had been a welcome diversion from what might have been a boring several months. She began to feel that perhaps the captain and the master chief had conspired with a little skullduggery of their own!

Hey! *Wait a minute*, this was no different than offering an extra credit question on the mid-term after you had already aced the test! She would have to have a little conversation with those two culprits and find out whose idea this whole thing had really been, and who had suggested using her as the Jill-of-all-trades to schlep all this stuff together!

She slipped into her costume for the production and hurried down to the crew's lounge to meet with the other half of the members of her cast and give them their draft letters to review. They would have a few minutes to modify and personalize them to their liking, before it was time to head up to the hangar deck. She felt a flush of victory as she collected the last of them. She would have them all ready for signature in the morning.

She stopped by the office to see how Fernandez was doing just as the captain was showing *Indy's* captain into his mess for dinner. He waved her over, "Captain Rolf this is Sam Wilson, she's the director of our show tonight. Sam this is Captain Tom Rolf, skipper of *Independence* and one of my oldest friends."

"Good evening Sir, welcome aboard and I hope you enjoy our production this evening. We've worked hard to make it a show you and your shipmates will enjoy."

Rolf shook her hand, "Great to finally meet you Sam."

She had no idea he knew anything about her, "Gosh Captain that's nice of you to say." She smiled impishly; "But you know Sir, I've been looking forward to meeting *you* ever since we got to the Med."

He chuckled, "It's hard to get through a meeting on this ship without someone mentioning the famous Sam Wilson for one thing or another."

Wilson laughed as he said it, "I'm sorry. I hope my infamy hasn't been a distraction. If you need anything while you're aboard Sir, just let me know."

She handed him one of the special show programs they had made to commemorate their turnover, the insignia of both ships were printed on the cover with the date of their anchoring together at Rota, and she asked him to autograph the program that all the admirals had signed the day before.

"It will be an honor Sam, they tell me that the show is the hottest ticket in town, I hope you taped last night's performance, you should send a copy to CHINFO, I'll bet they could use it in their recruiting and in their general navy PR."

She knew that their PMs who shot the video had played the show in the pilot's ready rooms too, via the ship's closed circuit TV system, it should be relatively easy to send a copy off to the CHINFO office in Washington. It would be a chance to showcase some of their shipmates and the incredible work they had put in to make the comic opera a fun entertainment for the whole battle group. And then she remembered the lost reel of *Gandhi,* maybe the CHINFO people would send the film of their show to all the other ships via the NMPX system. That would certainly make up for one little lost-but-eventually-found reel. "Thank you Captain, you've given me an idea. I have to go see to a few things now Sir, but I'll see you in our 'dress circle' tonight and I hope you enjoy the show."

He chuckled as she left and he thought out loud to Captain Christensen, "That girl is a dynamo! Where'd you get her from anyway Chris?"

Christensen nodded and smiled, "Luck of the draw Tom, I needed someone to take over real fast from the first class yeoman I was 'shit canning' for drugs and she had just reported aboard with zero experience, zero 'baggage' and that incredible smile. I snapped her up and she's been dynamite. C'mon in and have supper and I'll tell you how she saved my command for me."

The show, that evening on the hangar deck, was jammed with sailors from the inchopping battle group. The boat traffic that had begun arriving during chow time had been so heavy that the OOD had to set a special watch at the boom to direct traffic and prevent people from tripping over each other as they climbed the accommodation ladder. By 1900 there was an air of excitement on the hangar deck that made the previous crowds seem tame in comparison. Looking out at the sea of faces, as she prepared to welcome them and introduce the show, she was struck by one thing: there were hardly any women sailors in the crowd. *Indy's* battle group had a much smaller group of women crewmembers than *Ike's* had. She would have to find out why when she had a moment later on, but for now the show must go on.

"Admiral Lane, Captain Rolf, ladies and gentlemen of the *Indy* battlegroup, we are the Task Group Sixty Point Two Light Opera Company and we welcome you, *OUR RELIEFS,* to our production of Gilbert and Sullivan's classic comic opera *HMS Pinafore.* We'll have an intermission between the first and second acts and during that time there will be some libation made available." She paused and gave the audience her best Iowa-sunshine-girl smile, "For you sailors in the air squadrons that means *BEER!"*

The roar of laughter from the crowd almost surprised her and she had to laugh along with them, finally holding up her hand and stilling them, "Thankyou everyone, please enjoy the show."

From the first note of the overture until the closing strains of *He Remains an Englishman,* the cheers and laughs of the crowd inspired the cast of players to put on their best performance ever. The crowd applauded and laughed with the Tars, they yelled congratulations to Captain Corcoran, and they fell in love with Josephine and Buttercup. Sir Joseph blew them away and there was hysterical applause for his sisters, and his cousins—who he numbers by the dozens—and his aunts. The intermission was over before they knew it and Wilson's introduction to Admiral Lane and his staff was a delight. After the last curtain call, Master Chief Connolly joined her on the stage for their bow and he carried with him a bouquet of two dozen white roses. Wilson thanked him and took them into her arms. She'd never seen flowers onboard before and this tremendous bunch of them was almost a shock.

"Where did these *come from* Master Chief?"

"There's a card Sam, take a look."

She opened the tiny envelope wrapped in the tissue paper around the stems:

> Thank you "Sam" for everything
> you've done for me.
> Ens. Michael Nagle
> P.S. PN2 Stanfield told me white was your color

"My Goodness I certainly never expected anything like this just for trying to be a good shipmate Master Chief! Jeepers I haven't a clue where he got them."

Connolly chuckled, "I'm betting the navy exchange on the base at Rota doesn't have a single rose left Sam, maybe Sims has a vase or something you can put them in down in the captain's mess."

"Thank you Master Chief but I just thought of something else."

She gave a single rose to each of the sisters, the cousins and the aunts and had just enough left over to give one to Josephine, Buttercup and Hebe.

Admiral Lane and his officers thanked the cast for putting on such a wonderful entertainment and Captain Rolf patted her on the shoulder, "Captain Christensen says you're leaving when you get back to the states because you're headed to the naval academy. What I wanna know, is what I have to do to get a captain's yeoman like you!"

She laughed. "Captain any sailor can do any job, as long as they have the inspiration it takes for them to do it. My captain inspired me to do what he needed me to do. I just tried to do my best for him, and for my shipmates."

CHAPTER 19
LET'S GO HOME!

STANFIELD HUGGED HER FRIEND BEFORE *Porter's* boat got underway from the flagship to take her back to the destroyer she had called home for the last two and a half years. "Sam I'll meet you on the pier after we all tie up in Norfolk. We can catch the navy shuttle from the base to the airport together. I had supper with Teddy last night on *Montpelier* and then I kissed him goodbye. They got underway for New London, early this morning. Teddy's flying to Norfolk to meet us and we can fly to Iowa together. I'm so excited I can't even see straight!"

Wilson was excited too, "Oh Dorothy, me too! It's going to be so much fun! You can stay with me and my folks after we get home and I'll show you everything on our farm and in Corning. Dorothy I think it's the most wonderful thing I've ever been involved in! We'll have a great time and then we can fly to Pasadena for the wedding. Ron told me in his last letter that he would be flying in on the twenty second for Thanksgiving and he's as excited to go be Ted's best man as I am to be your maid of honor! Oh Dorothy I'm so happy for you both!"

Stanfield hugged her again, "Sam you and Ron are my best wedding present. My mom and dad can't wait to meet you both and they have a guest room for you when we get to Pasadena."

Wilson saw that the cox'n was anxious to back away from the boom, "Dorothy you'd better get aboard, I'll see you on the pier in twelve days. Oh here, please take my thank you note and give it to Ensign Nagle, it was nice of him to send me those roses."

Stanfield took the envelope from her, "I'll be happy to Sam, my mom wrote me that she and Teddy's mom have the guest list all worked out and almost all of Teddy's aunts and uncles are coming to the wedding. If Corning is as tiny as I imagine it, there won't be anyone left in town the day after Thanksgiving, they'll all be on the west coast for the wedding!"

Wilson gave her one last hug before the bowhook helped her over the gunwale and down into the launch, "Have a great crossing Dorothy! Say hi to Artie, Jimmy and John for me! Does your relief have it well in hand?"

Stanfield laughed and blew her a kiss, "My relief is a woman seaman, I took a page out of your book. I saw how great Marty was doing with you as her teacher and I picked a hard working girl sailor of my own!"

The cox'n gunned the engine as the boat backed away from the boom. Wilson waved and threw a kiss of her own as she called out, "See you on the pier in twelve days Dorothy, I can't wait!"

Wilson climbed the accommodation ladder and watched the boat bearing her friend until it crossed out of sight ahead of *Eisenhower*, on its way back to *Porter*. She had a torrent of different emotions as she watched. On one hand her best friends were leaving the battle group and heading off to new adventures and a life together. She would be leaving the ship and the people she loved too and the sense of loss was as palpable as if she was burying a pet. She would always look back on her time on *Ike,* with her shipmates and with the battle group as the best time of her life.

On the other she was going on to an exciting time at the naval academy and she would be near her love. He would most likely be in another company during their time there, but at least she would be near him and they could be together whenever the liberty schedule and their workloads would allow. She had tingles up and down her spine when she remembered how wonderful his lips felt against hers and how he made her feel whenever he held her tight. She knew that she had a lot of people who had great faith and confidence in her and she trembled when she thought of all that they had done for her.

They heaved in the anchor just after noon and Wilson watched from her station on the bridge with the Captain as the signal light on *Independence* began to blink out her farewell to them. She could make out the dots and dashes as the words flashed across the two miles of the bay of Cadiz to them: INDIA NOVEMBER DELTA YANKEE LIMA INDIA KILO ECHO SIERRA INDIA KILO ECHO: *"Indy likes Ike!"*

Captain Christensen began to chuckle as he watched the last of the signal come in, "What do you think Sam? Should we wish them luck?"

She had a better idea, "Gosh Captain I'm still in 'show business mode' and it would be bad luck to wish anyone that, especially the lead character. Why not send them: BRAVO ROMEO ECHO ALFA KILO ALFA LIMA ECHO GOLF!"

Christensen laughed and nodded, "Four Oh idea Sam!"

He beckoned to the OOD, "Lieutenant make a signal to *Indy*: 'BREAK A LEG' and then make: 'SAM SENDS'."

That evening on the mess decks her signalman friends were still laughing about it when she stopped by to say hello on the way to her table. "Hello everyone, how did our underway look from the signal bridge?"

SM1 Tegtmeier reached out and patted her arm, "Another classic signal Sam, I'm glad I had the watch when it was time to send it! I have a signalman buddy on *Indy* who probably busted a gut when he saw it come in. He'll probably try to one up us, but they don't have you aboard to give them inspiration."

Others stopped by her table to see her, shipmates whose lives she had touched in one way or another since she'd come aboard; her friend "Big Mac" McCutcheon the first class hull technician who had made the stainless steel deck braces to hold down her new Xerox machine and to thank him for his help she had helped him write a letter to his mother. Tammi Gilpin, the second class aerographer's mate who was now the coach of their women's basketball team stopped by and so did "Andy" Andaya, the Filipino third class mess specialist who worked for MS1 Sims. He wanted to thank her for helping him learn how to read English. It would make it lots easier to take the next MS2 exam if he could actually understand what was being asked, instead of just having to guess the questions *and* the answers.

She was feeling pretty terrific right about then and her tablemates saw it too, she was relaxed and even got a second helping of fruit salad. She wasn't rushing off to see to some detail of the show or check up on the final bits and pieces of their costumery. She had the biggest grin on her face and Bates was about to ask if she wanted to go a couple rounds with him before the movie when her whole demeanor changed in a snap. She was looking across the mess decks at someone and Bates immediately knew what she was thinking: "*Oh no* here comes the master chief again and he's headed right this way!"

He loomed over the sailors at their table and said the thing that Wilson would never have guessed. "Petty Officer Wilson, the honor of your presence is requested tomorrow evening at 1900 for dinner in the Chief's Mess. The invitation is made on behalf of all the members of the mess and the dress is service dress blue with ribbons. Don't worry Sam we won't make you give a speech, but we would like to have you celebrate the success of our Med deployment with us and we want to say goodbye, before you get inundated with other things."

Wilson stood up smiling as she took his hand in hers, she was almost as tall as the chief, "Master Chief I accept with pleasure and I do want to say something if that's okay with the mess."

She knew what an incredible honor it was, just to be invited to have supper in the Chief's Mess, she had chills just thinking about it. She would have to sit down tonight in her office and bang out some kind of statement, an address or something so she could let them know how she felt about them and what they had done to teach her how to be a good shipmate. That would have to wait until after Bates got his chance at her attention though. She was laughing inside as she thought about their upcoming bout.

The next morning the captain asked her to stay after the department head meeting. He waited for everyone to leave before he began, "Sam there is a rumor going around that you don't want to accept the award of 'Sailor of the Year' could you tell me why?"

"Captain I realize it's a tremendous honor and I'm grateful for even being nominated, but I'm leaving soon and I think that if I were to accept it, that would deprive another good sailor of the honor and I've already received so many honors aboard *Ike* it would be selfish of me to accept. Please give it to someone else Sir, a good shipmate."

Christensen nodded grudgingly, "You make a good case Sam, got anyone in mind?"

"Yes Captain I do, I think it should be HM2 Judy Obenauf, she's smart, a hard worker and as unselfish a sailor as I've ever met. I'll bet Dr. Cooley will nominate her if you ask him."

"I'll talk with him Sam, thanks. There's another thing I've gotten wind of too, there appears to be a sort of letter campaign going on having to do with a certain admiral's nomination for a third star and a fleet commander's billet. Do you know how that may have come about?"

She gave him something between a pout and a guilty grin, "Boss Congress has a couple more weeks of work before they go home for the holidays, I hope the Senate can push whoever it is in the navy that decides who goes where at the admiral level and then it should be a piece of cake to get him confirmed. I was the ringleader Captain, but I had almost two hundred eager accomplices. Every Senator is getting at least one letter and half are getting multiple ones."

She giggled, "And Captain, the best thing is, those letters won't sit in some staffer's in basket for two months, if I've learned anything from you it's how to use the wives' circuit and the warmth of home and family to move things along. I overheard Admiral Wilkins tell Admiral Morton that he is retiring at the end of the year and I think Admiral Townsend is perfect for the job. So I came up with the idea of a Senate letter campaign blitz. I even offered to visit my two Senators' wives and talk about it with them at Thanksgiving time."

Christensen just shook his head as he smiled and listened to the feisty and gifted sailor, "Sam I think your letter campaign is a great thing and you were right to do it. If you had asked me I would have advised against it but by golly it just may work! Did you ask the admiral what he wanted? Does his family have a voice in this?"

Wilson smiled, "I haven't said anything to the admiral Sir, but I did my homework. The admiral's wife is from Philadelphia and she's from an Italian family, I'm guessing she'll be fine with it. I didn't want to say anything to the admiral because he would have discouraged me because he wouldn't want to be involved in what he would call 'politickin'. I'm not saying anything to him unless he asks me either. I would like it to be a surprise when he's offered the job."

"Sam I think you are a pretty crafty sailor, I'm just glad you're on our side. I'd hate to go up against someone like you in a Russian sailor's uniform!"

Wilson was still laughing as she imagined herself in a Soviet sailor's kit, "Kapitansky that's the nicest thing you've ever said to me … I think!"

He chuckled, "Alright then it's Obenauf for sailor of the year unless you can think of someone else. I understand that you're dining in the chief's mess tonight."

"Yes Sir, I have to finish my little remarks, but I'm going to be there at 1900 as my father would say, 'in my best bib and tucker', and I'm going to enjoy myself."

He was smiling, "Good Sam, I can count on one hand the times I've been asked to eat with the chiefs and that's over a twenty two year career and plenty of ships. You're doing a lot better than I did!"

She laughed, "Gosh Captain, I'm excited I just hope no one

makes me feel homesick for *Ike*, If they do I know I'll cry and I don't want anybody to see me cry."

He patted her on the shoulder, "They won't Sam, and believe me, anybody that cries when they leave a ship that they love is okay in my book."

She arrived at the door to the chief's mess right on time. She'd taken special pains with her hair and had it pinned up on the top of her head, her best Betty Grable look. One more deep breath and she knocked. "Request permission to enter the chief's mess."

The door was opened immediately by Chief O'Connor who stood by in his blues and Wilson counted the gold hash marks under his E9 bo'sun's mate crow. There were eight of them and she thought, "My Lord, thirty two years the most I've ever seen, even Master Chief Connolly doesn't have that many!"

They were all there, all except for the handful who were on watch and couldn't come. Chief Thomas and Chief Peterson, Chief Owens and Chief Sutton were all there, along with the other eighty two chief petty officers between E7 and E9, and all of them were there to honor her and thank her for being a great shipmate. It made her think that any words she might say to thank them wouldn't be adequate.

She sat in the place of honor, just on the right hand of the master chief and they were all wonderful to her. Even though she only knew a handful of them very well, they all knew and respected her and they wished her well as she left for the next phase of her career. They told her sea stories and made her laugh and she realized that what Admiral Halsey had said about navy chiefs was true: they *were* what made the navy run and if you let them, they would earn your Navy Cross for you.

At last it was time, they were all looking at her and she knew she had to say something. She stood by her chair and saw that they were all looking at her with pleasant expectation on their faces. Well here goes, "Thank you all for inviting me tonight and thank you for the wonderful dinner. When the Master Chief invited me last evening I suppose I was more surprised than anything else and I thought I should think of something to say to express my gratitude, but as I thought about it I realized that all of you would much rather just have me say how I feel than listen to some fancy words I pulled from *Bartlett's* and embellished with the help of a thesaurus."

They were all looking at her with smiles now so she went on, "Chiefs I've only had the privilege of being your shipmate since February and I'll be leaving when we get to Norfolk. I'll be leaving a ship that I love and a crew that has welcomed me and chiefs that have helped me and taught me. I don't know what the rest of my navy career will be, but in the end I'll always remember that being here with you tonight, being invited to supper in *USS Eisenhower's* chief's mess, was the biggest single honor of my life."

They all rose then and applauded, they gave her certificates and a plaque and they each shook her hand and the women chiefs hugged her. Chief O'Connor even gave her a certificate making her an honorary "Irish Coleen". Afterwards she was able to make it almost all the way back to her berthing compartment, before she began to cry.

The rest of their transit to Norfolk went by for her in slow motion. She packaged up her mother's gifts and made arrangements with the postal clerks to ship them to Iowa. She reviewed the uniform requirements for women midshipmen and purchased the things she didn't have in the uniform shop. She was even able to find the insignia that turned her third class petty officer's dress blues into a woman midshipman's. She was well set up.

She had completed turnover of all her duties to Fernandez except for her job as ship's historian. She thought that Chief Thomas would be better at that, at least until Marty felt comfortable taking it over. The last official thing that she had to do was go over her final enlisted evaluation with the captain.

It was during that review that he invited her to have supper with him and the XO in his mess. He told her to come at 1900 too, just like the master chief had.

When she knocked that evening the door was opened by the

captain himself, and she found that the mess was full of officers that she knew very well. Admiral Townsend and his chief of staff, her friend Doctor Cooley and the air boss, Captain Sweeney, had all found time in their schedules to come and honor the woman sailor who had done so much to help each of them during their deployment. It was a nice surprise and she was unable to hide her sadness or her joy from them.

CHAPTER 20
LETTERS

WILSON TOOK HER LAST FEW hours aboard to write the letters she was delinquent on. The quiet of her office was assured because Fernandez was up on the bridge with the captain as the ship worked its way into Norfolk. Her first was to an old friend:

November 20th 1983
Aboard *USS Eisenhower* at Norfolk Va.

Dear Chief Berg,
    If ever I had dreamed my life would work out the way it has I would have never believed it. I'm due to depart from *Ike* tomorrow for a couple weeks at home in Iowa and I will be with my wonderful fiancé Ron there. After Thanksgiving I report to Annapolis and I'll begin the process of becoming an officer. I have no clue what they'll do with me between then and "Plebe Summer" but I'm sure I'll find something to do.
    You may have heard something about my friends Ted and Dorothy who so bravely saved a dozen young people and their driver in a rocket attack in Israel after our Naples port visit. I'm to be Dorothy's maid of honor when they get married later this month.

I'm sure your tour in Naples is going well and please give my regards and best wishes to your lovely wife. Her wonderful cooking is still a subject of discussion between Ron and me! My relief aboard is YNSN Marta "Marty" Fernandez, I've told her how much help you were to me when *Ike* was last in Naples and she has promised to stop by and say hello when *Ike* returns to Naples next summer.

Please stay well and safe,
Your friend,
Sam Wilson

She put in another sheet of paper and began the letter to her best friend that she hadn't had time to write before they got underway from Rota. She would give it to her in Norfolk before they caught the plane to Iowa.

November 20th
Aboard *Ike* in Norfolk

Dear Dorothy,

I know you are excited right now because of your upcoming wedding to Ted and I have to tell you that I am almost as excited about it as you are! I will be leaving *Ike* later today and I'll find *Porter* and we'll go together.

I can't wait to show you around our farm, it's right down the road from Ted's parents' and I have to warn you that when we get to Ted's house you will be mobbed by his family! All Ted's uncles, aunts and cousins are very anxious to meet you. My mom sent me a letter that I got just as we were getting underway from Rota. She said her friend Helen (Ted's mom) is almost dizzy with glee, now that she is finally going to meet you, be careful she doesn't crush you with her hugs and kisses! My mom says it's the most exciting thing to happen in our little town since the revenuers came and smashed up the "town still" during prohibition!

Thank you for asking me to be your maid of honor, I swear to you that I will be the best there is at it, just as soon as I read up on *what to do!*

I can't wait to see you again and I have a little something for you and Ted that Admiral Townsend gave me to bring just last evening.

My Dearest Friend, I can't wait to meet you on the pier!

Love,
Sam

There was another letter that she had to write before she could turn her attention to the men in her life:

November 20th
Aboard *Ike* in Norfolk

Dear Marty,

I've done my best to make sure you are ready to take over and give the captain *your* best. I have watched you progress and I am confident that you are ready, I think you will be better than I was and I'm sure you are over your shyness.

There is just one thing that I want to stress to you and that is that you must be sure that your conduct is totally above reproach. When people see you, they see you as an extension of the captain. You cannot afford to be seen doing anything that would bring discredit on him or the ship and you cannot put him in a position where he might be compromised. You have to think of him not only as your boss and captain but also as your brother, even your father. Captain Christensen is the best; give him all the help you can and when he gets relieved, as he will be soon, give his successor the same.

I'll be packed and gone by the time you finish lunch and by the way, I hereby officially give you my spot at my favorite mess table! Write me when you have a chance, I'll send you my new address when I'm checked in at Annapolis.

Your shipmate and friend,

Sam

Her next letter was to the man she was in love with:

November 20th
Aboard *Ike* in Norfolk

My Dearest Darling,

Please wish me luck today because I must leave this wonderful ship that I love, and if I cry when I do, it will be unmilitary, unseamanlike ... and unavoidable. I have made so many wonderful friends here and I know they all wish me well as I leave and come to join you at the naval academy. I will try to steel myself and pretend it means nothing, but deep in my heart I will be so sad and I will have to clutch some extra Kleenex in my hand as I walk down the brow.

I will find Dorothy as soon as I can and we will head to the airport together. I cannot wait to get home! I know my folks will love Dorothy and so will Ted's. I'm hoping you will arrive so very soon, so that we can be together. I will surrender Dorothy to the Manckowiczs and then I want to be with you, totally and completely with you. I want to take you to see all my cherished and secret things from when I was a little girl, and I want you to hold me and love me, and we will ride out on my horses to my secret hiding place in the thicket by the river.

Oh my sweet, sweet, wonderful Darling, I need you and I want to share everything with you, for the rest of my life.

Your adoring betrothed,

Sam

There was only one more and then she could shut off the word processor and lock up her office for the last time:

November 20th
Aboard the finest ship in the navy
Approaching Norfolk,

Dear Captain,

I thought that the hardest thing I'd have to do as I leave your ship would be to say goodbye to my shipmates on the mess decks. I had a chance to thank all the chiefs in their mess the other night and last night I was so surprised and so honored to be invited to have dinner with you, the XO, Captain Sweeney, the doctor and my favorite admiral. I will treasure that time together with all of you forever.

But I was wrong, the hardest thing for me is to try and say goodbye to you now on my last day aboard. You have been my leader, my teacher, my mentor and my friend for all these months and I have learned so many things from you. You have been an inspiration to me in everything and I only wish I could have been a better sailor for you, to have done more to make your job easier for you.

Please don't think I'm a crybaby but I *will* cry as I go across the quarterdeck later. They will be tears of sadness because I'm leaving, but they will be mixed with tears of joy, because I will be able to say that: "I was Captain's Yeoman on *Eisenhower* for the *best* Captain who ever lived!"

Sincerely,

Samantha Wilson, Mid'n USN

PS I will find out where your next duty station is and write as often as I am able. I have no idea what they will have me doing at the academy until I begin "Plebe Summer" but I have a few ideas I will suggest to the Superintendent.

SAM

GLOSSARY

AB (Aviation Boatswain's Mate): A navy rating whose members do all the "heavy lifting" on the flight and hangar decks of an aircraft carrier.

AN/AYA-8B: The sophisticated (and expensive) General Electric Corporation-built data processing and interfacing anti-submarine warfare system aboard a P3C aircraft.

ARFCOS (Armed Forces Courier System): A secure method for shipping large amounts of classified material from one command to another.

AW (Air Crewman): An enlisted member of an airplane's crew who operates a wide range of wizardly avionics equipment.

BCA (Broadcast Control Authority): The headquarters responsible for controlling a fleet broadcast including deciding what messages to send, when to send them and when to stop sending them.

BM (Boatswain's — pronounced Bo'sun's — Mate): A venerable navy rating that employs the finest of all the sailors. Shipboard they are involved in everything hard to do and / or dangerous.

BPDMS (Basic Point Defense Missile System): A quick reacting, rapid fire gun system designed to shoot down ("splash") an incoming missile or plane.

BQQ-5 (AN/BQQ-5): A digital submarine sonar system with both passive and active capabilities. It is standard equipment aboard modern US

SSNs and costs more than a thousand full-load Harvard college educations.

BuPers: Navy speak for the Bureau of Personnel.

Chop (Change of Operational Control): The navy's equivalent of going to work for a new boss. Also see "Inchop" and "Porkchop".

COD (Carrier Onboard Delivery): A small utility aircraft capable of launch from and landing on an aircraft carrier. These workhorses serve the carrier by hauling personnel, material and mail.

COB (Chief of the Boat): The senior enlisted man on a submarine. He is in charge of everything "crew" and reports directly to the Captain. Equivalent to a surface ship's Command Master Chief.

CHINFO (Chief of Information): The navy's head of public relations.

Crow: Navy slang for the spread-winged eagle just above the chevrons on a petty officer's rating badge.

EM (Electrician's Mate): A navy rating whose members maintain, and operate the equipment and circuits that keep the lights on and make the ship "go".

EMCON (Emission Control): A measure used to deny ones enemies the ability to track one by exploiting the electronic environment e.g. radar and radio signals.

EMO (Electronics Matériél Officer): The officer on a surface ship responsible for the operation and maintenance of the electronic equipment (e.g. radars, and other devices that break down frequently).

FICLANT (Fleet Intel Center Atlantic): The central clearing house where intelligence reports and sighting data are fused and evaluated and provided to the fleet via "INTSUMS", intelligence summaries.

FLN (Front de Libération Nationale): The communist-inspired party that defeated the French colonial government after a long civil war resulting in an autonomous Algeria.

Genser (General Service): The common ordinary everyday garden variety message traffic. It handles classifications between UNCLASS and TOP SECRET but excludes the SI (Special Intelligence) categories where one's eyes get burned out *before* reading.

GIUK Gap: The natural boundary formed by Greenland, Iceland and the islands of the United Kingdom. Any Atlantic-bound Soviet submarine has to pass through it and might be detected.

HM (Hospital Corpsman): The navy rating whose members provide health care to sailors and their families. They may be stationed ashore or afloat or even embedded in US marine echelons.

IC-Men (Interior Communications Technicians): IC-men operate and maintain a wide range of ship's electronic systems and on submarines are tasked with: care and feeding of the motion picture projectors and the crucial obtaining and maintaining of the crew's movies.

Inchop (and outchop): See "Chop". Inchopping ships relieve outchopping units so they can go home while the inchoppers shoulder the load.

JCS (Joint Chiefs of Staff): The highest level of military planning and tasking.

KCB (Knight Commander of the Bath): A British heraldic honor, conferred by the Queen, in the Order of the Bath.

LOFAR (and LOFARGRAMS): Low frequency and recording. A sophisticated means of acoustically detecting and tracking submerged submarines.

Maneuvering Board: A tactical aid used to compute speeds, directions and distances in conning a ship to its proper station in a formation of naval ships.

Maneuvering Watch: A special manning condition on a submarine used when leaving or entering port where each watchstation is manned by the most seasoned experts. It is equivalent to a surface ship's Special Sea and Anchor Detail.

MC (1, 7, 21, 24, 27 and others): Amplified shipboard communications systems.

Mess Cook (and often in jest, "Crank"): A junior enlisted person's temporary assignment shipboard. They assist the cooks with routine tasks and do the major cleanup of the mess decks.

MM (Machinist's Mate): A navy rating that operates and maintains a wide range of engineering main power plant systems including nuclear reactors, steam plants and auxiliary equipment.

MS (Mess Specialist): A navy rating whose members order and prepare the food for all hands.

NAPS (Naval Academy Preparatory School): A facility that prepares appointees for the academic rigors of the academy's classrooms.

NMPX (Navy Motion Picture Exchange): The distributor for films to all ships and naval stations.

Nuke: A ship powered by a nuclear reactor, also a sailor who has completed the rigorous training required by the "kindly old gentleman" and is qualified to operate one of the navy's nuclear propulsion plants. Finally, a weapon with a nuclear warhead.

OBA (Oxygen Breathing Apparatus): A portable appliance, donned by a sailor, which will supply him or her with breathable air for a limited time in a fire-and-smoke filled emergency.

OOD (Officer of the Deck): That officer on watch and responsible for the ship and all her actions.

P3C Orion: A land-based maritime patrol aircraft intended primarily for Anti-Submarine Warfare but employed in so much more.

PAO: Public Affairs Officer.

PK (Position Keeper): The part of a submarine's torpedo fire control system that keeps track of the bad guy and his relationship to you (the good guy!). Also the part of the system that breaks most often.

PM (Photographer's Mate): A navy rating employing personnel who take pictures and work in public relations and intelligence positions shipboard.

PMS (Planned Maintenance System): The navy's cookbook-style method of ensuring equipment wellness.

PN (Personnelman): A navy rating whose members provide a wide range of people-related services.

Porkchop (and often simply "Chop"): The Supply Officer. Thus dubbed by the slight resemblance of the distinguishing insignia of a Supply Corps officer to a fat pork chop, especially when viewed over the top of a beer glass in the officer's club.

PPI (Planned Position Indicator) Scope: A small, round amber-colored, analog display that shows the bearing to received underwater sounds.

PRD (Planned Rotation Date): An imaginary date established by the Bureau of Personnel for a sailor's departure for his or her next duty station.

QA-school: Quality Assurance school.

RHIB (Rigid-Hull Inflatable Boat): A small diesel-powered navy work and personnel boat carried aboard most warships.

RM (Radioman—now passé and replaced by IT—Information Systems Technician): Members of this navy rating are responsible for electronic communications.

Scuttlebutt: Navy slang for gossip. Historically a scuttlebutt was the water cask where the men on a sailing ship gathered to drink and trade rumors. It was the forerunner of the civilian world's office water cooler.

SH (Ship's Serviceman): A navy rating whose members provide a wide range of shipboard services including running the ship's store, the laundry and dry cleaning equipment.

SLJO (Shitty Little Jobs Officer): The officer routinely tasked with the time consuming, the boring and the insignificant jobs that otherwise would bog down the XO and the department heads.

SM (Signalman): A navy rating whose members communicate between ships with semaphore and flag hoist during the day and flashing signal light at night. Salts often refer to them as "skivvywavers".

SMAW (Shutdown Maneuvering Area Watch): A watchstander who tends the shutdown nuclear systems and the electric plant on a submarine when in port.

SSIXS (Submarine Satellite Information Exchange System): A high-speed, satellite-relayed transceiver system enabling a submarine to communicate rapidly and reliably.

TACCO (Tactical Coordinator): The naval flight officer who directs the traffic and controls the resources among a P3C's acoustic, radar and other sensor operators.

TDU (Trash Disposal Unit): A submarine's garbage disposal. Essentially a scaled-down vertical torpedo tube, it is filled with weighted trash and "shot" when needed.

XO (Executive Officer): The second in command of a navy ship. He assumes command when the Captain is disabled, or on leave.

YN (Yeoman): A navy rating whose members specialize in written communication, maintain files and provide administrative service shipboard and ashore.

ACKNOWLEDGEMENTS

The author extends his grateful thanks to:

My classmates from the Huntley High School, Huntley Illinois Class of 1963 who leant their names to many of the characters in this tale.

My Pal, the great Dr. Jim Holden who encouraged me to write this series, graciously read over the first draft of the manuscript and taught me what to do, if I run into a big pain in the ass.

My Pal Ernie Perkins (CDR, USN) (Ret) who kept the VP chapters honest.

My little brother Jim (CDR, USNR) (Ret) who knows a thing or two about A6s and carrier decks.

Ms. Amy Hallberg for keeping the French, bien.

Ms. AC Proctor of Essex Graphics for the nifty cover art.

MC2 Julia A. Cooper for the photo of Ike used in the cover art.

"All Hands Magazine" for the photo of sailors in their blues used in the cover art.

My best friend of all these 50 years, my wife, Gail Palmer.

OTHER BOOKS BY THE AUTHOR

Find them all on Amazon.com in Kindle or paperback format.

Raghats!
A tale of the navy … not just any 'ol sea story!

The Hut Line
A novel of Aruba.

The "Liberty Series"
The Liberty Launch
"The stupid shall be punished."
(A Seaman Sam Wilson story)

Aegean Liberty
"What's a Grecian urn?"
(A Sam Wilson story)

Dungaree Liberty
"Sailors do get even."

Coming Soon

Vampire Liberty
"Take tomorrow off Sailor!"
(A Sam Wilson story)

The Liberty Risk
"Nobody can be *that* dumb!"

Made in the USA
Columbia, SC
03 November 2023